The Window

The Window Duet Book One

Angie Lee

ISBN: 9798838829870
Printed in the United States of America
First Printing, 2022

Dedication

This book is dedicated to C., who told me I could do it, over and over again until I believed it, too.

Also, for Rhonda and Don. I hope you guys are proud of me, and please watch over Alex Lee.

Special thanks to Debbie M. Flanagan, Tracey & Jolie Frazier, and Stefanny M. Chaisson.

Table of Contents

PROLOGUE

My hands were slick with blood, but I finally wrenched the door open. I spilled out onto the front porch, bruising my knees as I collapsed onto the rough wood. I screamed, "Help me, help me! Oh my God, somebody, please help me!"

I prayed for someone to hear my cries and come to my rescue. I frantically searched the street but saw no one. I hugged myself with as I sobbed incoherently, my cheek throbbing with pain.

I could feel the blood running down my face, mixing with my tears, before dripping to the floor beneath me. "Please help me!" I screamed again and again.

PART ONE – BEFORE

CHAPTER 1

Guilt is a strange thing. It's neither constant nor absolute.

Guilt is the scale on which you place the weight of your sin, holding your breath as you wait for the needle to decide between "What have I done?" and "I had no choice."

~

The first time I took my clothes off for him was an accident.

I wasn't any kind of siren or seductress. I was a stereotypical housewife and mother of two, the kind you see on sitcoms on any given weeknight.

Before everything that would happen, I had believed myself to be a decent person. My days consisted of taking care of my family, cooking, housekeeping, and running errands. I wasn't out there looking for excitement or drama. I couldn't even make the excuse that the drama had found me.

Yes, I was to blame for all of it. Yes, I probably made some wrong choices, but you know what they say about hindsight.

Had I known then how it would all end, I'd never have let myself be drawn into his game.

CHAPTER 2

Dear Diary,

Most people would probably call me a bored housewife, but I'm not. I hate that term. I'm a housewife, and yes, sometimes I'm bored. But when the words are put in that order, it seems so... I don't know... selfish. After all, what woman wouldn't like to be a stay-at-home mom? I know I'm blessed to be included in that category.

It's just that now that Kara is older and Jason has gone off to college, I get lonely and sometimes restless. You can only go on so many shopping trips before you have everything you could ask for. And I do.

I'm not a neglected wife, either. Even though sometimes it feels like I am, that couldn't be further from the truth. Grant does nothing but dote on me. All I have to do is point to something and say, "I want..." and whatever it is, Grant's hurrying to get it for me.

To prove my point further, I just have to look outside at the massive SUV that he bought me to celebrate my fortieth birthday. It sits in the driveway, a shiny reminder of how charmed my life is. I didn't even have to ask for it.

The car just showed up the morning of my birthday, complete with a gigantic red bow. The unveiling was a spectacle that drew the neighbors from their homes.

So, you see, if anything, I'm spoiled, not neglected.

K.

CHAPTER 3

It started on a Wednesday, which began like any other weekday in my adult life.

I'd been doing yoga in the basement gym for over an hour. My thoughts were drifting, here, there, nowhere. I was idly thinking of how much I missed the long lazy days of summer when my children were out of school for three months and were spending most of their time at home.

The three of us, Jason, Kara, and I would often go shopping in town or to see a movie, but most summer days, we'd hang around the house, swimming, napping, playing cards, or cooking together while we waited for Grant to join us at the end of each day.

With Jason in college now, I knew those sorts of summer vacations would soon be coming to an end.

Jason would get his degree in a few years and start his career. He had warned us that he planned to move away from us after graduation. Jason dreamed of seeing the country and yearned to meet new people and experience new places.

I'd be sad to see him go, but I was proud of the man he was growing up to be. Never one to dwell on unhappy thoughts, I tried to shake off my melancholy mood.

I completed my routine, switched off the music I always had playing during my sessions, then turned off the soft overhead lights and left the gym. I was flushed and sweaty, and my muscles felt pleasantly loose. I climbed the steps to the main floor, glad to be done with exercise for the day.

On the way to my bedroom, I detoured to the kitchen to grab water from the fridge. I pressed the chilled bottle to my forehead as I continued through the living room and down the hall.

I smiled at the family photos lining the walls and touched a finger to our wedding photo before starting up the stairs.

I pulled my shirt away from my damp body and grimaced. I was in desperate need of a hot shower. I was also toying with the idea of sneaking in an afternoon nap before Kara came home from school.

Raising a teenage daughter was exhausting, to say the least. Kara was thirteen going on twenty-five, a mix of childish energy and volatile adolescent emotions.

On any given day, she was just as likely to have me in tears as make me laugh. At times, I'd do both at once as the result of a single conversation. I never knew which version of my daughter would climb off the school bus each afternoon, and I had to be prepared for either one.

I reached the top of the stairs, pausing to look around our bedroom. This room was my favorite one in the house.

The whole upper floor was mine and Grant's, designed loft-style, and it had always been my sanctuary. We had a sumptuous bathroom with double vanities and an antique clawfoot tub, with enormous his-and-her walk-in closets and expansive windows overlooking the backyard.

I adored everything about our home.

Grant dabbled in architectural drafting, one of his many talents, and he had designed our home to resemble a classic Victorian on the exterior. The house sported gingerbread siding and wide porches, but Grant had added more updated elements here and there, mainly in the bathrooms and kitchen. I'd spent hours scouring antique shops for the crystal doorknobs on the bedroom and bathroom doors.

The living areas were illuminated by a huge wall of windows that ran down the length of the backside of the house. My ultramodern kitchen would delight any professional chef.

Once in the bedroom, I sat on the tufted bench at the foot of my king-sized bed and peeled off my sweaty socks, tossing them into the hamper in the corner.

I could feel the soreness in my thighs as I stood up. I pushed my leggings down my legs, wiggling my butt from side to side to help ease them down. This was no easy feat; my workout outfit was still damp with sweat. My tank top followed my pants into the hamper.

Lastly, I pulled my sports bra up over my head. As the thick material cleared my line of sight, I happened to glance out over the yard through the open window blinds.

Our bedroom was on the backside of our house, facing the large yard. The windows were wide, tall sheets of glass, reaching from the floor to the ceiling, duplicates of the ones downstairs.

On a regular day, the view would be lovely and serene, including the brick patio I'd laid with my hands, our sparkling blue in-ground pool with its waterfall feature and attached hot tub, and beyond that, the neighbor's wooden fence that separated our yard from his. Near the fence, the neighbor had two ancient oak trees on his side.

The trees, while lovely to look at, were constantly dumping leaves and acorns in my pool. However, today my gaze was met by a startled pair of eyes looking up at me.

As in, much, much younger than myself. Probably around my son's age, which only made this situation worse.

I had just flashed my forty-year-old breasts at a gorgeous young stranger.

To be fair, I must admit that the "girls" still looked surprisingly good for my age, if I did say so myself. Maybe they weren't nearly as perky as they were when I was twenty, but for being in my fourth decade, they weren't in bad shape. They still sat up high, which was a miracle considering I had carried and nursed two children. I've been told my legs, long and shapely from my daily yoga and barre routines, were my best feature.

Most of the time, I still considered myself attractive, which I mostly accredited to the hoard of creams, lotions, and potions I religiously applied twice a day to fight off fine lines. Bi-monthly visits to a ridiculously expensive hair stylist had allowed me to keep the flaming red hair of my youth, which I wore in long, loose curls that reached nearly to my waist.

Still, I saw the signs of aging, especially on the thin skin of my hands. If I straightened my fingers, the skin of my hands resembled a map made up of wrinkles.

My mother's hands were now my hands. Regardless of my looks, I'd always been a modest woman. I didn't wear my tops too low or my shorts too high. I dressed appropriately for a middle-aged mother of two.

I certainly didn't make a habit of exposing myself to handsome young men.

But back to my current situation... I mean, humiliation. I mentally cursed myself for not closing the blinds before changing out of my clothes, but in my defense, all I'd usually see in the neighbor's yard was his fence, the top half of the damn oak trees he was so proud of, and the occasional squirrel.

Curious, I risked a quick peek through the very edge of the window, keeping most of my body behind the curtain.

He was still there, looking at my window, his huge grin on display as he stood still on the top step of the ladder. He held the tree trimmer in his hands, but he'd switched it off at some point.

Once again, I ducked behind the wall, awkwardly stretching out one arm to pull the cord that would close the blinds and block his view into my bedroom. Resting a hand over my racing heart, I stayed well hidden without a clue as to what to do next.

The one thing I was certain of was that I was not going to look out of the window again until I was sure he was gone.

CHAPTER 4

Later that afternoon, I was standing at the kitchen island, prepping dinner and daydreaming a bit as I chopped and sliced.

I wondered who the man outside might be. Was he a relative of my neighbor or just a hired worker? Either way, it was unlikely he'd be there again tomorrow; the trees didn't seem to need much work done.

From my post in the kitchen, I heard the front door slam loudly, vibrating the walls, and I shook my head. Kara knew how much I hated when she slammed doors.

I could always gauge her mood when she came home just by how loudly she would make her entrance. Here lately, even if she'd had a good day or was just in a rare, pleasant mood, she would make as much racket as possible for no reason other than to annoy me.

I heard her drop her book bag on the wooden floor in the hall, making more unnecessary noise.

Years of experience with Kara had taught me that I must choose my battles with her wisely. I decided not to comment on the noise she made, and I went back to chopping onions. *Just let it go*, I told myself.

Reprimanding Kara would only cause an argument in which one of us would end up either shouting or stomping out of the room, and I had other things on my mind today.

I felt irrationally guilty about my earlier unintentional peepshow, so I was doing self-inflicted penance by making Grant's favorite dinner, hamburger steaks smothered in gravy with green beans and garlic mashed potatoes.

Not that the meal would undo anything. "Hey honey, I showed my breasts to another man today. Would you like some more potatoes? Here, have some gravy, too."

I rolled my eyes at my silliness as Kara came stomping into the kitchen, feet pounding the floor in her heavy combat boots. Her recent penchant for clunky shoes and an all-black wardrobe was another cause for our regular arguments.

I'd learned to hold my tongue regarding her clothing choices, but I drew the line when she told me she wanted to dye her beautiful hair black. That was one of the very few arguments we ever had that she didn't win.

Kara plopped down on one of the bar stools at the island and spun her seat like a child, her long locks whirling around her face as she turned.

I had a flashback to when she used to spin on the swings at the playground. She'd turn until the chains were twisted and then let go, laughing as she turned in circles. I smiled at the memory.

My daughter was lovely, though she'd hate me saying so. The red hair she inherited from me framed a heart-shaped face, complemented by her clear porcelain skin and a cute dusting of freckles across her nose. She hated them and insisted on covering them with heavy foundation anytime she left the house.

"What's for dinner?" Kara asked instead of a greeting, her stool making one final rotation before slowing to a stop.

She snatched a carrot from my chopping board, another habit she knew I disliked. I was always worried I'd accidentally cut her with my knife when she reached for something on the board.

I resisted the urge to roll my eyes at her and instead replied, "Hello to you, too. My day was fine, thanks. How was yours?" with a hint of sarcasm.

Catching my tone, Kara did not show the same restraint. She sighed dramatically and replied, "Hi, Mom. My day was fine, too. So, what's for dinner?"

I ducked my head to hide my grin. It would start an argument if Kara saw it.

She'd automatically think I was laughing at her.

"Your dad's favorite, hamburger steaks, and mashed potatoes."

Kara's face formed a mask of horror. "God, Mom, do you seriously not know how many carbs are in that? There's, like, thousands."

Based on her reaction, you'd have thought I told her it was worms and snails for dinner.

Again, I tried not to smile. Why did carbs matter to Kara today but not yesterday when she'd eaten a small mountain of French fries with dinner?

Before she could make any further commentary on my dinner choices, the front door creaked open once more.

We heard a hollow thump, followed by a low curse. "Shit."

My husband was home, and not for the first time. It sounded like he had tripped over Kara's book bag.

Grant came into the kitchen and reached over to ruffle Kara's hair.

"Hey, kiddo. Keeping Mom company?"

She pulled away and shot him an exasperated look.

He, too, had wisely chosen not to mention her book bag. Many late-night discussions had been had about her bad habit of leaving her things strewn about the house. But between dealing with one of her meltdowns and her book bag issue, tripping and falling seemed to be the lesser of the two evils.

I admired my husband from my spot at the island. Grant was aging nicely. His hair was dark and thick, only lightly sprinkled with silver at his temples. Well over six feet, he had a trim figure, narrow at the hip, broad at the chest.

Like me, he spent hours in our gym, trying to stay in shape. The five o'clock shadow lining his jaw only added to his appeal.

Grant set his leather messenger bag and phone down near the door, then came around the island. He leaned over and kissed me on the cheek, as was his daily habit before leaving for work and when he got home.

I grabbed him by the shirt and pulled him in to deepen the kiss.

My husband tasted like peppermint and home.

Predictably, Kara made a disgusted face at our display of affection but kept her opinion to herself for once.

"Hey, babe. How was your day? Do anything fun?"

He also snagged a carrot from the board. Did they want to lose a finger?

The chopping knife slipped from my hand, clattering to the granite countertop.

"Oops!" I said as I swiftly picked it back up. "Um… no. Nothing fun, same old stuff. You know, the usual."

I was babbling, and I knew it.

Desperate to change the subject, I chirped, "Look, I'm making your favorite for dinner!" My voice squeaked on the last word, and Grant arched a brow at me in a silent question but thankfully didn't comment.

"It looks amazing, love. Do I have enough time to grab a quick workout and shower before we eat?" he asked.

I hoped he couldn't see the relief on my face. I knew my cheeks were flaming, and I wanted him out of the kitchen.

"Absolutely, take your time. I'm nowhere near done here. Go on, get out of here."

"I'm going. I'm going. I know where I'm not wanted."

Grant gave my butt a playful swat as he walked past me and out of the room, headed down to the basement.

I breathed a sigh of relief as he disappeared. *Get it together*, I told myself. *You're acting like an idiot.*

CHAPTER 5

Before you go making assumptions, let me set the record straight, I love my husband very, very much.

Grant is a wonderful partner and a terrific provider, and my kids couldn't ask for a better father.

He and I enjoy spending time alone together, and we still have a healthy sex life.

I have no complaints in that department, and I've always considered myself lucky that he chose me all those years ago.

To most people outside looking in, my life is one most women would kill to have.

Grant and I started dating halfway through high school. Ours wasn't your fairytale football- star-and-head-cheerleader love story. Quite the opposite, in fact. He and I were both introverts, awkward, bookish, and happiest when left alone. Grant was obsessed with computers, me with science.

Neither of us fit in with the jocks or the cool crowd, nor did we want to. In our junior year, the two of us were partnered for a project in Biology.

I had always known Grant; in our small town, you usually went from kindergarten through high school with the same batch of kids. Occasionally a student would leave the school or join a class mid-semester due to their parents' job transfers. Otherwise, you'd likely see the same faces until graduation.

While I did have a small circle of girlfriends I liked to hang out with on weekends, I had almost zero experience with the opposite sex. I was shy and sensitive, self-conscious of my bright red hair and braces. The mere thought of holding a conversation with a boy would make me stammer and blush, another curse of being a natural redhead.

Grant was much the same as me. From age seven, poor eyesight forced him to wear thick glasses that he had to constantly push up his nose. He much preferred spending time in the computer lab tinkering with programming to hanging out with other boys his age. Sports held no interest for him.

After spending hours at each other's homes working on the bio project, Grant and I first became good friends, bonding over the homemade cookies my mother brought us during each session.

We discovered we enjoyed many of the same movies and books, trading our favorite graphic novels between us. Coincidentally, we were both only children of our respective parents.

Gradually, we fell into the habit of spending most of our free time together, and as we grew older, our relationship progressed naturally from there, as they often do.

By the time we started our last year of high school, Grant and I were solidly established as a couple. Right about that time, his body filled out, transitioning from knobby knees and elbows to wiry muscles. He'd gotten a better haircut and contact lenses; suddenly, girls noticed his gorgeous blue eyes.

I, too, had blossomed. My curves came in, and I started experimenting with makeup and hairstyles, letting my hair grow long.

These physical changes did not affect our relationship. We only wanted each other. Grant and I were each other's best friends and confidantes. We became lovers shortly after the beginning of our senior year, laughing as we fumbled under the blanket in the back of his father's truck. I knew Grant was the one for me, and he felt the same.

The two of us spent many hours planning for what we'd do after graduation, talking about what our future would be like. He was going to apply to a technical college specializing in computer technology. Computers were his passion.

As for myself, I wanted to be a pediatrician, like my father was, and my father's father had been before him. Then, of course, there'd be the natural progression to marriage and a white picket fence, then babies and happily ever after.

We applied to colleges nearby, not wanting to be separated for four years or longer if I got into medical school, and we were both accepted to our first-choice schools.

After we graduated, Grant and I rented a tiny one-bedroom apartment halfway between our two campuses. Life was very good; everything was going the way we had planned. We worked hard to earn our degrees, we were right on track for Grant to graduate, and I was already researching and applying to medical schools. We both took part-time jobs to help with the rent and school expenses that our financial aid and scholarships didn't cover.

Then, suddenly, everything changed. Our future took a hard left turn and became less certain.

It happened near the end of our third year of college. I'd felt unwell all weekend, nauseous, and fatigued, but I assumed I had caught a stomach bug or I was simply exhausted from my full course load and working a part-time job every evening after classes.

I had stayed home from my shift working concessions at the movie theater and was huddled on the sofa under a blanket, sipping hot peppermint tea while I waited for Grant to get home from his after-school job.

Finally, I heard Grant's key in the door, and he came in with his arms laden with books and fast-food bags. Kicking the door shut behind himself, he came over to the sofa to kiss me.

"Hey, babe, how are you feeling? Any better?"

As he leaned towards me, the smell of fried chicken and onion rings drifted up to my nose, and I bolted off the sofa and ran to the bathroom.

A couple of hours, a trip to the drugstore, and three positive tests later, we reluctantly accepted that we were pregnant. Shortly after we broke the news to our parents, we decided to move in with Grant's parents to save money while he finished his degree. They were more than happy to have us.

After we settled in the basement apartment they gave us, I tried online classes for a few weeks. I was too sick from my pregnancy to keep up with it, so I withdrew from school. I reasoned that I could always return to college after the baby started kindergarten.

For the sake of practicality, I set aside my girlhood dream of having a huge fairytale wedding, and our parents arranged a simple but sweet ceremony at the courthouse shortly before the baby came. I didn't want all my friends and family to see me in a wedding dress with a huge stomach, anyway.

I never made it to medical school. We had a new baby, Jason, then shortly afterward, a new house, and Kara followed a few years later.

After Grant graduated, he quickly found a job he loved in his chosen field. He got in on the ground floor of a start-up IT company and worked his way up the ladder there, from intern to management, finally reaching his career peak as vice president of development. His dreams had been realized.

As for me, I stayed home with the baby in the house Grant had designed and built for us. For now, at least, my dreams of being a doctor were on hold. Midnight feedings and diaper changes had eclipsed them.

For months, I slept most nights in a rocking chair in the nursery with Jason, not wanting to keep Grant awake. His office hours were long, and he often fell asleep in his chair after an exhausting day at work.

All of this was to explain how I got to the point where I was restless, and maybe a little resentful, and looking for something different to happen. And then it did.

CHAPTER 6

My life was much the same from day to day, so I started the next morning as I usually would. Early mornings were dedicated to yoga or barre routines in our home gym, and I spent the rest of my days doing various things for my family.

I made doctor appointments, paid the bills, shopped for groceries, and cooked the meals. I shuttled Kara to soccer practices and picked up Grant's suits from the cleaners. It was monotonous at times, for sure.

As a little treat for myself, at least once every few weeks, I tried to arrange a girls' lunch with my best friend, Angie.

A nurse practitioner and single parent of two teenagers, she was always on the run, but she tried her best to set aside some time for me when she could. I also tried to be considerate of her limited free time, so most of the often, I'd prepare a girls' lunch at my house and have it ready when she arrived.

Angie blew in the front door like a tornado for that day's visit. Barely topping five feet, she was a small woman, probably no more than a hundred and ten pounds. Even with her demanding schedule, Angie always looked perfectly put together, her hair done, and her makeup in place. Delicate and feminine, with golden blonde hair and blue eyes, she resembled a China doll. But you'd only mistake her as such one time. Despite that girl-next-door exterior, she was a chain-smoking, rough-talking ball of fire.

Angie and I met in college, both working part-time at the same local movie theater and instantly became close. In the slower hours, after one movie started and before the next one began, she and I formed a close bond, munching stale popcorn mostly because it was free and chatting about our college classes and boyfriends.

Our friendship survived into our adult years, despite our post-college lives taking drastically different paths. I had no secrets from Angie, our bond surviving time and distance.

Today I rushed her through the customary hugs and kisses that were the norm at the start of each visit.

Any other time, we'd begin with questions about how the kids were doing in school, how Grant's job was going, and other mundane topics like the weather or the high gas and grocery prices. There was no time for that today. I was dying to tell Angie about my accidental strip tease and couldn't wait to hear her take on it.

I ushered her straight into the kitchen and waved her onto one of the stools at the kitchen island. I planned how to begin my story as I dished up the lunch I'd prepared ahead of time.

I'd made chicken salad with walnuts served in crisp lettuce cups, a meal I knew she loved, then added a pretty plate of fresh-cut fruit for us to share.

With a flourish, I set one of the plates in front of her.

She looked down at it and hummed appreciatively. "Kat, this looks delicious, as usual. Come sit and eat. You look a little stressed today. Is everything all right?"

I knew I didn't look my best. I'd been too distracted that day to put much thought into my appearance. I poured us half a glass of chilled white wine and carried my plate to her side of the island to sit next to her.

I was anxious to tell my tale, so I popped a berry into my mouth while I waited for her to start eating.

I swallowed the fruit, and after taking a deep breath, I began.

"I need to tell you something, and it's pretty wild."

Angie set her fork down and arched one perfectly trimmed eyebrow. After she swallowed her bite, she blotted her lips with her napkin and asked, "Something wild, huh? You and Grant try a new position?"

I choked out a laugh. "Well, no, but it did happen in the bedroom."

After all these years, I was used to her off-color commentary.

I proceeded to tell Angie the whole story, starting at the beginning with my exercise that morning and ending with me pulling the blinds closed on the stranger.

When I was through with the story, I waited eagerly for her to speak, expecting Angie to be shocked and scandalized.

She was neither.

Angie sat looking at me for a minute without speaking.

After a long pause, it started getting awkward, so I waved my hand in front of her face. "Hello, earth to Angie, is anyone home?"

She cracked a smile and said in a breezy tone, "Oh, I'm still here. I was just waiting for the rest of the story."

Wait. What?

I was confused by her reaction. Wasn't that enough?

"What do you mean, the rest?" I asked.

Angie leaned over and lifted the wine bottle. She carefully refilled our near-empty glasses before answering me, her tone gentle. "Kat, here's the thing. It's not like you did it on purpose. You were just changing out of your clothes, and some guy saw you with your top off. There's no crime in forgetting to close a window. Don't take this the wrong way, but it's not that big of a deal, you know? You'll probably never see him again. Even though I'm sure you made his day." Angie paused and waggled her brows at me. "Maybe you and Grant should try a new position if this is your definition of a wild time."

Just then, her phone rang, and she excused herself to take the call after letting me know it was one of her kids calling.

I sat there quietly, mulling over her words. As I stared at the half-eaten food on our plates, I felt a small sense of relief. Angie's reaction wasn't what I expected, but maybe she was right. It was possible that I had made something out of nothing, and it truly wasn't as big a deal as I thought.

That man wouldn't be interested in me anyway. He had to be at least twenty years younger than I was. I estimated he was around Jason's age, maybe a few years older.

He was probably off with friends, laughing about it over a beer.

CHAPTER 7

After lunch, Angie left, and I puttered around the kitchen, putting away the leftovers and loading the dishwasher.

Once I'd had time to think about what Angie said, it made perfect sense. It was not like I had cheated on my husband or anything like that.

The guy was just in the right place at the wrong time. Or the wrong place, at the right time, depending on how you looked at it.

That was all it was, a chance encounter, no more, no less. There was no reason to feel guilty.

So why then, did I fight the urge to run upstairs and look out to see if he was there?

Forcing myself to stay put in the kitchen, I wiped my already sparkling countertops and started a grocery list. Eventually, I found myself with nothing more to do.

I spent the next few hours on my laptop, looking for new recipes to experiment with and making sure the kids' tuition bills were paid for the month.

Despite these attempts to distract myself, my mind kept wandering to the stranger.

Why did this insignificant encounter have me so disturbed? Was I that starved for attention?

Annoyed with myself, I tried to focus on something else —anything else. It struck me that I should finish my degree, so I decided to sign up for classes and take them online or at night until Kara graduated.

Jason was in college, and Kara would be starting high school the following year, so there was truly nothing keeping me from pursuing my medical dream anymore. My family needed me less and less every day, and I reasoned that people went back to school in their forties all the time.

Yes, that's what I'll do.

With a renewed sense of purpose, I clicked into a web browser to look for local classes.

~

Despite my pep talk to myself and what Angie had said, I still couldn't let it go. It was as though the whole encounter had let something loose inside me, and I had no idea how to put it back.

If I was honest with myself, I did want more out of life. Not a different life, just more in this one. I was unfulfilled in some ways and wanted to feel like the old Kat again. I would have liked to be something in addition to being a wife and mother, something more than the housekeeper and errand runner.

As soon as I admitted this to myself, guilt flooded me. So many people would consider themselves lucky to have what I had. I knew just how fortunate I was. Also, I knew what could happen when restless wives started feeling as I did.

But I didn't want to have an affair. I had a great marriage and a solid partnership with Grant. I just wanted… something.

CHAPTER 8

Something showed up that Friday.

The house was quiet. Kara was in school, and Grant had gone to work. Jason wouldn't be coming home until the weekend.

I was upstairs in the bedroom, straightening the bedclothes and organizing my closet shelves, humming along with the radio when I glanced out the window.

The man was back in the neighbor's yard, as delicious as I remembered.

He was up on the ladder, and I could see his muscles flexing as he lifted the heavy trimmer above his head. Shirtless again, his arms and back glistened with sweat in the morning sunlight.

My goodness, he was beautiful. He looked like the model on the cover of every medieval romance novel, minus the long, flowing locks and the chainmail.

Ever so slowly, so my movements wouldn't catch his eye, I inched over to stand behind the curtain, leaving the blinds open.

I had a decent view of him, but I hoped he couldn't see me. I'd be mortified if he caught me admiring him.

Thankfully, the man didn't look in my direction. He just kept working on the tree, muscles bunching and relaxing. It was mesmerizing to watch.

I'm not hurting anyone by looking, I thought. It was no worse than watching a hot guy on a television show.

Grant worked hard to keep in good shape, but let's face it, his body couldn't compete with a much younger man's.

I didn't know exactly how much time had passed, but it was at least a quarter of an hour. Looking away from the spectacle seemed to be an impossible feat.

Over and over, *I'm not doing anything wrong,* I repeated like a mantra in my head.

I was busy admiring his stomach muscles when suddenly he lifted his hand in a wave.

My gaze shot up to meet his, and I saw that he had been able to see me, and now I'd been caught ogling him.

My cheeks burst into flames. I knew I was busted, and since nothing I did now would change that, I lifted my hand to return his greeting.

Acknowledging the gesture, he shot me a sexy grin, nodded once, and then turned back to his work.

Looking back, I believe that his wave and smile led me to do what I did next.

It didn't bother him that I was staring. He might have even been flattered by my attention.

Gathering my courage in my hands, I shifted again, centering myself in the window to watch him work. I had a clear view now, and it was an excellent one.

He glanced up at me after a little while, and I caught his smirk before he returned his attention to his task. *This isn't hurting anyone*, I told myself again.

CHAPTER 9

He was out there working most days over the next two weeks. I spent as much time in my window as I could get away with. There was no more hiding behind the curtain. I enjoyed watching him, and for some reason, he seemed to enjoy watching me. It was a mutually beneficial arrangement.

When he saw me, he'd smile and sometimes give me another little wave. I'd come to look forward to these little interludes, and I knew I'd be sad when he finished his job there and moved on.

I wouldn't say I was obsessed; intrigued would be a more appropriate word.

Outside the time I spent in the window, life went on as usual. My son, Jason, came home from college for the weekend with his hamper full of dirty clothes in tow. Knowing he wasn't going to take care of them, I directed him to leave his laundry basket in the utility room as soon as Jason came through the door.

This was our routine. He knew to collect his clothes from there: washed, dried, and folded before returning to campus on Sunday.

I tended to spoil my kids, especially my firstborn. I could deny him nothing, not that I tried very hard.

Jason had been a fussy newborn after a long and difficult labor. He didn't sleep through the night for months as other babies did.

As I mentioned, I struggled in my role as a new mother and wife, especially with Grant working so hard in his new career.

I was grateful those days were behind me now. My son had grown into a tall and handsome man with his father's eyes and athletic build.

In the most secret and shameful part of my heart, I knew Jason was my favorite of my children, though I'd never admit that to anyone.

I loved Kara, don't get me wrong, and I would do anything for her, but she tried me in ways her older brother never had.

Jason dumped his duffle bag and laptop in his room and wandered back to sit next to me in the den. Settling in, he propped his booted feet on the coffee table, earning a stern look from me.

"So, what's been happening, Mom? Meet any hot guys lately?"

He dropped his feet to the floor and grinned at me, and I was startled, then shook my head at him.

I knew he was messing with me, but the timing of his little joke could have been better. "Absolutely, a new guy every day," I retorted as Grant entered the room.

Grant set his beer on the table and asked, "Who's got a new guy every day?"

I groaned. Bad timing, again. What was with these men today?

"No one does. Your son is pretending to be funny. Get Kara down here, and let's go get some Chinese."

As I waited for my family to pile into the car, I couldn't help but wonder if I'd see the man the next day.

CHAPTER 10

It happened like this.

Two days later, I came up from the basement after my yoga routine, again hot, sweaty, and looking forward to a shower and a late breakfast. I kicked off my shoes in the laundry room and headed down the hall to the main stairs again. I'd be lying if I said my steps weren't a little more hurried than usual. Something in my belly fluttered with anticipation.

As soon as I walked into the room, unable to stop, I went straight to the window to see if the man was out in the neighbor's yard.

Yes.

There he was, looking back at me as though he'd been waiting for me.

I held my hand up in greeting as my heart pounded in my chest. But this time, instead of waving back, he did something that surprised me. He gestured to his chest and then pointed at me.

Not understanding at first, I looked down at my shirt, and then I put up my hands to show him I didn't get what he was telling me.

He mimed slowly, taking off a shirt, and again pointed at me.

My jaw dropped. Did this young, gorgeous man want me to take my top off for him?

Was it some kind of a joke? He had to be making fun of me, this sad old lady who stood around watching him work every day.

But no, he stood there smiling encouragingly while I tried to figure out his motive.

Could I do it? Should I do it?

The answers were clearly yes, I could, but by no means did that mean I should.

I absolutely should not take my top off in front of that window. What I should do is flip him off and close the blinds.

But I didn't do that.

Before I could think twice about what I was doing or the possible consequences of doing so, I slowly reached for the hem of my tank top and peeled it off my damp body, keeping eye contact with him as best I could.

I stood there and waited, trembling a bit in my yoga pants and sports bra, and I saw that he was no longer smiling. He was watching me so intently; it was as though I could feel the heat of his gaze on my body, touching my face, my belly, and my chest.

His lips were slightly parted, and his hands were fisted at his sides.

I was appalled as I realized what I'd just done, so I reached out and tugged the strings that would close the blinds.

He disappeared as though he'd never been there at all as if I'd imagined the whole thing.

CHAPTER 11

This went on every day for four days. By the third day, however, I had skipped my daily workout and was pacing the kitchen until it was the time I'd usually finish and head up to the bedroom to shower and change.

How was I supposed to concentrate on exercise, or anything else, when this man was waiting to see me? I knew by now he was absolutely waiting for me to show up.

My rational brain knew I was headed down a dark and dangerous path. I could hardly think about anything else. My every thought was consumed by what I did in the window.

Still, I went through the motions with my family, sitting down to dinner with Grant and Kara, laughing at their jokes, and making conversation. All the while, my mind was on the man outside.

I justified it, thinking that what I was doing wasn't really that wrong because I didn't know his name, had never exchanged a single word with him, and didn't intend to.

The Window

Every morning, I kissed my husband goodbye and all but pushed him and my daughter out the door to work and school before rushing to change into my yoga clothes.

By this time, I could tell the stranger was dragging out the tree work, making it last as long as possible. He had finished trimming one tree and moved on to a second one, but he was working much more carefully and at a slower pace than he had on the first few days.

On the last day, he gave up even pretending to work and left his tools in the grass, unused and forgotten. He was standing in the yard, waiting.

Waiting for me.

That day, however, something changed. Taking off my shirt had started to feel almost normal after doing it a few times. But after I'd removed my tank top at his request, he gestured to his pants and then to me.

My breath quickened, even as I told myself that there was no way I would remove my pants in front of a stranger, especially a hot young one.

I had barely finished this thought, and then I was scrambling to remember what kind of underpants I had put on that morning.

Please don't let me be wearing granny panties, I thought, already knowing I would do it.

Madness, that's what this is.

However, the warmth curling through my lower belly told me I wanted to yield to his request.

I hadn't felt this instant arousal in years, not since Grant and I first started dating.

Grant. I refused to think of him now. I tried to block his face from my mind.

With no further hesitation, I hooked my thumbs in the waistband of my pants and slid them down my legs.

CHAPTER 12

Dear Diary,

In my dreams, he speaks to me. In my dreams, he calls me Katherine. I don't know his name. Even if I knew it, I wouldn't write it here.

Grant can never find out about this. I can't believe what I've done. A stranger asked me to take off my pants, and I did it.

Who am I? This isn't me, is it? The look on his face as my pants hit the floor is something I'll never forget.

It was like I could physically feel his eyes on me as he repeatedly looked me over from head to toe. He smiled at me and slowly nodded his approval, pleased with what he saw.

Writing this down, my body is responding as though it's happening all over again. After I took off my pants, I stood there in my bra and panties (thankfully, a cute pair), somehow all my earlier self-consciousness disappeared.

Is what I did so bad? There's a thin line here between right and wrong. I don't know the man, I've never spoken to him, and I don't even know if he'll be there from day to day or ever again.

On the other hand, the fact that I can't tell anyone, except my diary, about it confirms that it's absolutely wrong. I don't want to imagine what my husband would say if I told him what I'd done.

What I do know is that I want to do it again.

The way he looked at me made me feel things I thought my body had forgotten. I want to feel that way again.

I'm not overly worried about being caught. The area is quiet at this time of the day, most people have day jobs, and the neighborhood kids are in school. The guy who lives behind us is a traveling life insurance salesman, so he's rarely home on weekdays.

It seems that it's just me and this man, alone in the little world we've created.

K.

CHAPTER 13

I indulged in a few tears of self-pity as I wrote this entry.

I wanted to tell someone. I wanted to confide in Angie. I believed she would never betray me, but at the same time, I couldn't bear to see judgment written on her face or, worse, disgust. Angie's opinion of me mattered too much.

No, I decided, I definitely couldn't tell her. The risk was too great. Angie's strong sense of right and wrong may have outweighed her loyalty to me. I was already risking my marriage. I couldn't add my relationship with my best friend to the list of things I was putting on the line.

CHAPTER 14

Dear Diary, I feel so alive.

If the world were to end tomorrow, I'd want to die feeling just the way I do right now. I don't know how my family is so oblivious to the changes in me. Every time I look in a mirror, my cheeks are always flushed, my lips seem plumper, and my eyes are brighter. I make breakfast for Grant and Kara with a smile on my lips.

There's a new bounce in my step each morning because I know that in just a few short hours, I'll put on my yoga outfit and arrange myself in the window for his pleasure and, I must admit, mine.

I'm burning inside already, just thinking of his dark gaze brushing my bare skin like a lover's caress. His eyes seem bottomless, a deep, dark pool of secrets that he's waiting to share with me.

There's just something about the way a man looks at a woman...

K.

CHAPTER 15

The man was inarguably stunning, from his ebony curls down to his flat stomach. I looked but could find no imperfections. I'd had plenty of time to inspect all the parts I could see while he stood gazing back at me.

Maybe I was looking for a reason to stop what we were doing. In the dark of night, I came up with a dozen valid arguments as to why I should put an end to this and not stand in my window for him the next day.

But in the light of the morning, I found more ways to justify why I should. After spending time in the window, the rest of my day seemed to pass more quickly. I'd find myself leaning on the counter, staring dreamily at nothing.

Glancing at the clock, I'd be surprised to see half an hour or more had gone by while I was lost in my thoughts of him. I'd catch myself running my hand down my neck and across my chest, imagining his dark, dark gaze touching me in the same places I was touching.

I stopped at every mirror I passed, trying to see myself as he saw me.

CHAPTER 16

Dear Diary,

When I spend time in the window, it's almost as if I'm in a dream state.

The sharp, defined edges of the real world become softer and blurred. Time doesn't seem to matter as much.

Another change today.

After I had taken off my clothes, as I had done before, he lifted his hand and spun one finger as if to say that he wanted me to turn in a circle. He'd never done that before, always seeming satisfied to view me from the front only.

I almost didn't do it. My backside isn't my best side, you know. But seeing the plea in his eyes wore down my reserve. I sucked in my stomach and spun slowly around, allowing him to see my whole body.

I'm not sure if these full-length windows are a blessing or possibly a curse, as there was no hiding anything in the bright light of the morning. I think he approved of what he saw, though, because when I came back around to face him, I saw his tongue dart out and lick his lower lip. Seeing his reaction sent a bolt of fire straight down from my heart to my center.

These feelings are so intense, almost indescribably so.

I'm not replacing parts of my life. I'm enhancing them. It's like adding salt to your dinner. There's nothing wrong with the food, but adding the salt just makes it... better.

I've always done what's expected of me my whole life. First, I did what my parents thought was best. Then I did what Grant and the children expected of a wife, a mother.

It's finally time to do what Kat wants.

K.

CHAPTER 17

I found myself worrying that he'd grow bored with our game and disappear. After all, he wasn't doing anything more than looking at me. I wasn't ready for this to end. I had to do something to prolong our time together.

Saturday, I made some lame excuse to Grant of having errands to run in town. For the past few days, I'd been dropping casual hints about needing to update my wardrobe.

Grant was on his way to the office for yet another weekend catch-up session. He was checking emails on his phone as he gathered his things to leave, and he hardly seemed to be listening to what I was telling him about my plans for the day.

He pecked me on the cheek as he walked out the door, not bothering to look up from his phone.

"Okay, have fun, spend lots, love you," he mumbled, and then he was gone.

I wondered if some part of me had secretly hoped Grant would push me for details on where exactly I was going, whom I was seeing, and what I was buying.

Is it possible I was looking for an opening to confess it all to him? Maybe I needed a reason to call off this shopping trip.

I shrugged. It was too late now, at any rate.

After Grant left, I wandered down the hall and knocked gently on Kara's bedroom door. I didn't open it. She hated when Grant or I did that. We had to wait until she responded with permission before we could go in.

Instead, I called to her through the door. "Honey, I'm going to town to pick up a few things." As an afterthought, I added, "Would you like to go?"

As I waited for her to respond, I silently prayed, *Please, please, let her say no.*

With my luck, this would be the one occasion she'd want to spend time with me.

But I had to ask. My relationship with Kara was already in shambles. If she decided she wanted to go with me this time, I'd put off my secret mission until she was back at school the following week.

Her voice came from behind the closed door. "No. I'm busy."

There was a pause, and then, "Hey, Mom, wait. You could bring back pizza. Pepperoni and extra cheese. Dad said he probably wouldn't make it home before we have dinner, and I'm getting kind of tired of your cooking."

Her last comment was unnecessary and designed to hurt. The barb hit its mark, but again, I chose to let it go.

I considered making a joke about carbs to see if I could make her laugh.

I didn't because she never did.

I'd pick up the pizzas on my way home, and maybe we could have a nice dinner together, just the two of us.

After assuring her I would get what she wanted on the pizzas, I skipped up the stairs to my bedroom, humming a little to myself, excited about my secret mission.

CHAPTER 18

I drove for almost an hour before I pulled my car into the parking lot of an upscale lingerie boutique two towns over.

I'd gone further than usual because I was afraid I'd run into someone I knew, and besides, there were no stores in our town that would carry what I was looking for. It had to be the exact right thing.

Shifting the car into park, I gathered my purse and keys, locked my car, and walked across the lot to the discreet entrance to the lingerie shop.

My stomach trembled with excitement. I had been thinking of this for days, how I'd surprise the man with what I planned to buy today.

Inside the store was a pink and white lingerie wonderland. Everything was pristine: the floors, the walls, the display tables, all in various shades of blush and cream, hot pink and ivory. Here and there were low benches wrapped in pink or cream satin.

Mannequins were dressed in any outfit you could dream of, ranging from sickeningly sweet white lace confections perfect for a virgin's wedding night to black crotchless teddies complete with studded collars. I idly wondered if they sold whips, too.

There was no chance I'd be buying one of those. What if Grant accidentally came across it?

I shuddered as I imagined trying to explain that purchase to him. I envisioned trying to convince him it was a Halloween costume and chuckled.

I wandered slowly among the display tables and racks, brushing my fingertips on the smooth silks and satins when I spied a red lace bra and panties set and removed it from the rack.

Glancing around to ensure no one was nearby, I held it up against my body. Ashamed even as I did it, I envisioned myself wearing it for him... and Grant.

I felt guilty for even thinking of putting it on for both men, but I did. I could imagine the look on either of their faces if they saw me in it.

I was absolutely going to hell.

I browsed the entire store, deflecting the bouncy blonde salesgirl twice. The first time she approached me, her demeanor set my teeth on edge.

I admired a long cream-colored nightgown edged with lace at the hem and neck. It looked like something out of an old black-and-white movie, very vintage.

The girl came up to me smiling with all her teeth; there had to be ten thousand dollars' worth of veneers in there.

In her grating little-girl voice, she addressed me. "Hello, ma'am. Are you shopping for yourself or your daughter today?"

I wanted to smack the smile right off her smug face. Did I look too old to be shopping for lingerie?

Instead, I forced a gracious, if not quite friendly, smile and replied, "For myself, thanks. I don't need any help right now. I'm just browsing."

I turned my back, dismissing her. I'm generally not rude to salespeople, but this girl had my hackles up.

She huffed a bit and then left to resume her spot behind the desk.

My mood was somewhat deflated after that interaction, but I was determined not to let her ruin this experience for me.

I returned to one of the front display tables and picked up a tiny, midnight blue lace thong, thinking it would go nicely with my pale skin and red hair. I flipped through a nearby rack until I found a pushup bra that would match perfectly.

I took my selections up to the register, hoping a different employee would be able to ring me up.

No such luck.

The girl glanced down at what I had chosen and lifted her eyebrows just the slightest bit before fixing her customer service smile.

Almost hoping she'd comment, I held her gaze, forcing her to look away first. The rest of the transaction was quick.

The salesgirl was probably ready for me to leave the store so she could go back to playing on her phone. I hadn't bought that much, so her commission would be small, and I was sure she was bothered by my attitude.

Taking back my credit card, I snatched my bag from the counter and swept out of the store.

CHAPTER 19

Back at the car, I put my bag in the backseat and shut the door.

As I turned to get into the driver's seat, I heard someone call my name.

"Kat? Kat Browne, is that you?"

I froze. I had driven out there to avoid running into anyone I knew, and now I was trapped.

I put on yet another fake smile and turned. I did a mental facepalm when I saw who called my name.

This couldn't have been worse. It was Stacey Sheridan.

Her husband, David, worked for Grant on the development team at their firm, and we occasionally met up and did things with them as a couple, like going out to dinner or having them over to the house.

David was a nice guy and had a lot in common with Grant, but Stacey was the biggest gossip in our circle of acquaintances.

If there was anyone I didn't want to see today, it was her. She'd be on the phone with David the minute she returned to her car.

Stacey came across the parking lot to me, teetering on her high heels. She loved to wear high-heeled shoes, but the poor thing had no balance. She had to lean on the side of my car for support.

I tried not to show my annoyance when the metal handles of her bag scraped my shiny paint.

"Kat, darling," she said in her breathy little-girl voice, "I thought that was you! What on earth are you doing way out here?"

Lucky for me, it had taken her so long to get over to me in those shoes that I'd had time to make up a story. "A friend of mine is getting married, so I was getting a little something for her to wear on her honeymoon."

I gestured vaguely behind me toward the lingerie store.

"Oh, anyone I know?" she asked with a little smirk.

I guessed she didn't believe the "buying for a friend" explanation I used.

"No, probably not. Just a girl I met through Kara's soccer team's moms' group."

I tried to change the subject, "So, how have you been? You look amazing, by the way. That dress is killer on you."

Thankfully, it worked. Stacey's favorite topic was always Stacey.

She tossed her highlighted extensions and gushed, "Thanks! I got it at this adorable little store David, and I found when we went on a weekend trip to the mountains a few weeks ago. Oh my gosh, you and Grant should go! We stayed at this wonderful bed-and-breakfast. Our room was so romantic, with the best view, and the food was so good! I swear I gained five pounds!"

Stacey droned on about their trip for a few more minutes. I tried to look interested in what she was saying, but I couldn't wait to get away from her.

Finally, I made a show of looking at my watch. "Gosh, look at the time. I'm sorry, Stacey, but Kara is waiting on me to bring her some pizza, and she gets so cranky if I'm late. Kids, huh? Call me soon?"

Visibly annoyed at being interrupted, she nodded. "Sure, Kat. We need to get together for drinks and dinner again soon. I'll let David know I saw you, and I'll have him get with Grant to arrange it, okay?"

Shit. I had to think fast. "Sweetie, please don't tell David you saw me out here. My… um… my car's been making a strange noise, and Grant told me not to take it far until he has it looked at. I don't want to get into with him, but I was dying to come take a look at this shop for my friend's gift. Be a darling and let's keep it our secret, okay?"

Stacey loved secrets almost as she loved herself, so she agreed.

To my absolute horror, she held one of her pinky fingers out to me.

"Pinky promise?" she said, with a wink.

Much to my shame, I linked my pinky finger with hers and responded, "Pinky promise!"

I felt like a ten-year-old girl, but I was so ready to be rid of her that I'd have done nearly anything.

We said our goodbyes, complete with double air kisses, and she headed back the way she had come, still in danger of falling over.

Relieved, I waved at her back and got into my car.

My lies were piling up. I would have bet Stacey was on the phone with David that minute. I'd have to hope David would forget about it and not say anything to Grant.

Although, my chances were fair because no one listened to everything Stacey said. It was impossible.

CHAPTER 20

Dear Diary,

It's Monday. Two days had gone by since I'd seen him, and I was nervous, but he was back. I'm ashamed to admit that he was all I thought of all weekend.

When I should have been paying attention to Grant as he told me about a new program that he had gotten approved for market, the man was on my mind. When I should have been helping Kara with her book report, I thought of him and what we'd do this week, wondering if he'd be open to something different.

I found myself praying he'd be there and hoping he wouldn't have finished his work. Thankfully, he was out there right on time. To surprise him, I didn't put on my yoga clothes this morning. Instead, I put on the pair of lace-edged navy-blue bikini panties and matching push-up bra I bought. I covered them with my robe and belted it tightly. I'd wavered back and forth a few times, unsure about changing our routine, but the look on his face when he saw me in my robe assured me that I'd made the right choice.

As I stepped into the window, his eyes widened, and he grinned his huge white smile. A moment later, he gestured to his waist and then to me. I knew he wanted me to undo the tie. I took it in my hands at both ends but didn't pull it yet. Instead, I smiled at him playfully, making him wait for it.

I was in charge. I was powerful. I could see him watching expectantly, but he didn't move or make any more gestures. The delay seemed as pleasurable for him as it was for me.

More later, I think I hear the school bus. *K.*

CHAPTER 21

Dear Diary,

Where was I?

Oh yes, I was teasing him a little by not undoing my robe right away. Instead, I stretched the moment out, not wanting the anticipation to end too soon. How long, I can't say for sure, but soon I couldn't delay any longer.

I wanted him to see what was under my robe. I wanted to watch his reaction as he saw the surprise, I'd prepared for him. Mostly, I wanted to see his desire for me spread across his face. I watched him lean forward as I gently pulled one end of the tie and then the other, causing my robe to fall to either side, leaving a gap in the middle. There was just enough space between the two sides where he was able to see my panties and the swell of my breasts above the lace cups.

His eyebrows rose, and his lips parted. He nodded encouragingly at me, so I rolled my shoulders and pushed my chest out, forcing the robe to fall to the floor behind me. I stood naked but for the tiny lingerie set and let him look his fill. I raised my chin and threw my shoulders back, pushing my chest out.

Growing bolder, I looked down at my body and ran my hands down my sides and past my waist to my hips. Then ever so slowly, I walked my fingers back up my belly and stopped just beneath my breasts. I lifted my eyes to his, asking a silent question. He understood at once and gave me one quick nod, his gaze intent.

I cupped my breasts in my hands and gave a light squeeze, causing them to push up out of the cups slightly.

He was almost panting by then, and I felt like a goddess. I may have only been with one man in my whole life, but my effect on him was unmistakable, and I basked in how it made me feel.

K.

CHAPTER 22

I constantly reminded myself that my window time wasn't my real life. It was just an interlude, a brief moment where I could do something to please myself and no one else.

I kept telling myself that everyone had a hobby; this was mine.

Some hobby, huh?

One night I was distracted at dinner, and Grant noticed. He had apparently tried to get my attention more than once and finally reached over and cupped my face in his hand.

He turned my face to look at him, which I hated.

"Kat? Did you hear Kara? She's talking to you." Grant frowned at me as he said this.

He knew how quickly Kara would turn on one of us if she was displeased or felt slighted.

Annoyed, I brushed his hand away and turned my attention to my daughter. Kara's face was crossed with annoyance.

"I'm sorry, sweetheart. What were you saying?" I asked her.

"Mom, what is with you lately? You're always staring at the walls, and you don't even respond when we say something to you half the time. Are we, like, boring you or something?" she asked sarcastically.

I felt the color rise in my cheeks. Kara wasn't wrong; I hadn't been listening to the conversation at the table. I'd been lost in thought, planning tomorrow's outfit, and hadn't heard a word she said.

While I was absorbed in my thoughts, my family had been discussing a sleepover Kara wanted to go to.

"I really am sorry." I looked sheepishly from Kara to Grant and back. "I just have a lot on my mind right now. I'll do better, I swear."

"Whatever, Mom." She sighed again and angled her body toward her father, effectively excluding me from their conversation.

This was just another mark on the side of the list of reasons why what I was doing was so, so wrong.

CHAPTER 23

Dear Diary,

For him, I choose my poses carefully, the ones that showcase my best assets and hide what I consider my imperfections. I imagine myself in a boudoir photoshoot and mimic those positions.

I never sit. I stand, I lean, I lounge against the window frame. I bend a knee to lengthen the line of my leg and show off my firm thighs.

I flatten my palms against the cool glass so that the heat of my body leaves a damp handprint, temporary proof of what I've done that will soon disappear as if it never existed.

It's disgusting and shameful for me to even think this, but in a twisted way, Grant sort of benefits from what I'm doing. By the time he gets home from work, I'm so aroused from my time in the window that I can't wait to get him into our bed each night. I count the minutes until dinner is over and Kara is safely in her room for the evening, and Grant and I can be alone.

I'm pretty sure Grant has noticed my sudden renewed interest in sex, but he hasn't commented on it, choosing instead to enjoy this new me, whatever the reason may be. If Grant wonders what has brought about this change, he doesn't ask. He just reaps the benefits.

At night, in the privacy of our bedroom, it's like he and I are teenagers again. We're trying new things, having sex that lasts longer and is more exciting than it's been in years.

I've ordered some new lingerie online and can't wait for the outfits to arrive so I can wear them. For Grant and… him. I do feel guilty because I know in my heart that what I'm doing is wrong.

But God help me, I can't stop. It. Feels. So. Good.

I don't feel the pain in my feet from hours of standing. I don't notice the ache in my arms from holding them above my head for an hour or longer. These small discomforts no longer matter.

All that matters is how he sees me.

K.

CHAPTER 24

I rolled off Grant, panting heavily, and fell back on the pillows next to him as he turned his head to look at me and said, "Jesus, Kat, what's gotten into you lately?"

"You, obviously," I replied wickedly, making him chuckle.

I rolled over onto my side and propped my head with one hand, leaning on an elbow.

One eyebrow raised, I asked, "Are you complaining? Because I could stop, you know, if you didn't like it or something." I was kidding, giving him a hard time because I could.

I sat up and slid to the end of the bed.

"Like it? Jesus, Kat, I loved it. You were amazing." He was still breathing heavily, and his body was covered in a fine layer of sweat.

I looked over at his naked body as he lay on the sheets. I admired his classically handsome profile, straight nose, and full lips. Grant was a stunning man. Then I stood, allowing him a view of my butt as I looked around for my robe.

Grant's hand snaked out and grabbed my wrist, yanking me backward until I fell onto the bed with him.

I laughed at his playfulness. I loved it when we were like this, happy and connected.

"Oh, no, you aren't going anywhere, Mrs. Browne," Grant warned me, pulling my head down to meet his kiss.

See? I was doing this for Grant, too. All I had to do was keep telling myself that, and one day maybe I'd believe it.

CHAPTER 25

Dear Diary,

I'm crushed. I dressed up for him and took my place in the window, but when I opened the blinds, he wasn't there. In my underwear, trembling and nervous, I waited. At least an hour had passed. I repeatedly searched to the left and right to see if he was in a different place today, but he never came to me.

I didn't realize how addicted I had become to what I was doing, how much I craved the feeling of freedom this gave me.

Where is he? Will he be back? I have to stop here; I have to get dressed to meet Angie downtown for lunch.
K.

CHAPTER 26

The timing of Angie's lunch date offer couldn't have been any better. It was like she somehow knew I needed a distraction that day.

When she texted and asked if I could get away for lunch, I jumped at the opportunity. Her schedule seldom allowed us to go out somewhere. This made me wonder what had happened that gave her extra time today, but I wasn't about to question her.

I relished the thought of sitting at a table somewhere with Angie, chatting and sipping a fruity drink while someone served me for a change. If I had to stay alone in the house for another day, I'd end up checking the window obsessively to see if the man would appear.

I didn't want to do that. I wanted to be the one in control of my feelings and my actions. It was beginning to feel uncomfortable how disappointed I was when he didn't show up.

In a way, I could feel myself slowly becoming addicted to spending window time with him, and I didn't like how that felt.

The Window

To lift my mood, I dressed in a green halter-style sundress that tied around the neck and added strappy gold sandals. This shade of emerald-green set off my pale skin in a striking way.

I brushed out my hair and added a bit of lipstick and mascara to complete my look. Unlike Kara, I didn't feel the need to cover my freckles with makeup. I thought they were becoming and gave me an air of youth.

Grabbing my keys and purse from the table in the foyer, I slipped on my oversized sunglasses and left the house.

CHAPTER 27

A little while later, I sat in a cozy booth in a new, trendy café that doubled as a bookstore. It was a cute little place, selling books on the left side and serving a light lunch menu on the right.

I idly looked over the food choices while waiting for Angie to arrive. The menu consisted of what Grant would call "chick food."

There was a decent selection of tea sandwiches, soups, and light salads. The list of desserts was more extensive and decadent. The triple chocolate brownie with caramel sauce sounded divine.

I wondered if Angie would split it with me.

Or... I could take one home for Grant and me to share later, preferably in bed. I smiled at the idea.

Just thinking of Grant made me feel better. He'd been working long hours lately and most weekends. I missed him.

I loved the closeness we'd enjoyed lately due to the new confidence I'd found in myself and my body. It was strange to think I had the man outside to thank for that.

The door to the café opened, and Angie swept in, turning heads as she did so. As always, she looked amazing. Her hair was freshly highlighted, and her makeup was perfect.

I was glad I had put a little extra effort into my appearance that morning. It was hard to shine next to Angie. It would have been easy to hate her if I didn't know what an honest, loving person she was.

Angie leaned over and kissed me on both cheeks before sliding into the booth across from me.

Right away, she saw that I had already ordered her favorite peach tea and smiled up at me as she sipped from the straw.

"Delicious! Thank you, honey, you're so sweet."

She took another sip and leaned back against the padded leather of the booth. "So... what's new with you? You look gorgeous, by the way. I love that color on you."

I wanted so badly to confide in her, to get her advice. Maybe not the whole story, but I wanted to tell her how I felt more purposeful, more confident. However, I realized I couldn't do that without telling her how I'd come to be feeling this way. She would never accept less than the whole story.

I settled on a semi-truthful version.

"Well, let's see. Things are going pretty well, I guess. The kids are fine, Jason's doing great in all his classes, and Kara is... Kara. You know how I struggle with her. Besides that, Grant and I are in a good place right now. We've been trying to spend more quality time together the last few weeks, especially at night."

I gave her a meaningful look and went on, "I think it's given me a boost I needed. I had been feeling kind of blah about myself and about my life for a while."

Angie reached over and patted my hand. "You are not blah. You, my darling, are spectacular!"

I burst out laughing. Sometimes Angie could be over the top with her compliments. It was nice to hear those things now and then, though.

"A co-worker of mine, Beth, went on a couple's cruise with her husband last month, and they both loved it. You and Grant should look into it. I could ask her for the name of her travel agent if you want it. Beth told me since they've gotten home from the cruise, she and her hubby have been doing it like rabbits," she told me, leering at me over the table.

I was intrigued by the idea of a couple's cruise. It would give Grant and me more time to reconnect away from home and the kids. Jason could come to stay at the house with Kara while we were gone. I could already hear her whining that she was too old for a sitter and could stay on her own.

Another dark thought intruded.

What if I didn't show up in the window for a whole week? Would he go away and never come back? To my dismay, the thought of never seeing him again made my stomach turn.

Lost in thought, I barely registered the waitress as she brought our lunch orders to the table. I forced my attention back to Angie, but she was staring out of the window to the street beyond.

As I unwrapped my silverware, I noticed she was frowning slightly, so I asked her what was wrong.

"Something wrong with the food, Angie?" I asked, taking a bite from my plate.

Angie glanced back at me and replied, "I swear there was a guy out there staring at us through the window." She squinted to see better.

Stunned, I turned to look but didn't see anyone I recognized.

Could it be…? No way. We had never seen each other outside of our window time.

Besides, how would he know where I was?

Still, I wondered.

"What did he look like?" I asked her, trying to sound nonchalant.

She finally pulled her gaze away from the window and sipped tea before answering. "Well… He was gorgeous. Young, dark, built. Just the way I like them. Maybe I should go out and try to find him."

She chuckled at her joke. I tried to laugh with her, but inside I was reeling. I knew exactly who could fit that description. He had to have followed me there.

But then, why hadn't he shown up in the yard this morning? I felt flattered but also apprehensive. It gave me a rush of feminine power to know that he was interested in me, but did I want him to be interested enough to follow me?

No, I definitely wasn't comfortable taking this… whatever it was, out of the backyard.

It was a little too much.

Angie had already forgotten about him and had started telling me a story about a set of twins that had come into the clinic a few days back.

I tried to put the man out of my mind and pay attention to her. I'd think about him later.

For the rest of the meal, we chatted over our food, sharing bites of my Thai salad and her club sandwich as Angie caught me up on her life and her kids. She'd met a nice guy on a popular dating app and said he seemed to have potential that she thought might be going somewhere. They'd been on five dates, and Angie planned to ask him back to her house the next time her kids were with their father for the weekend.

I hoped it would work out between them. Angie deserved nothing but the best.

I was disappointed when lunch was over, and Angie had to leave. I missed her so much between visits and was always sad when our time was over. However, Angie had her life to return to, and so did I.

We hugged goodbye and vowed to text later in the week.

No sooner than I was back in my car, I thought of the man outside.

Buckling my seatbelt, I resisted the urge to speed home and check the yard. I chastised myself for acting like a teenage girl with a crush. *I am a grown woman, and I will behave like one*, I thought with determination.

I wouldn't go anywhere near that window when I got home.

CHAPTER 28

Dear Diary,

He came back! I don't know, and probably never will, why he wasn't there yesterday.

It doesn't matter, though. The relief I felt when I saw that he had returned this morning has left me feeling uneasy. It can't be normal or healthy for me to react this way to his absence. It's as though I've become somehow dependent on my times in the window.

I have a whole life outside of what I do with him, and that's my real life, not this. Whatever it is. This is just… something I'm starting to need, like I need air to breathe.

Sometimes I wish I was a poet or a songwriter. Then maybe I'd have the words to describe the feelings that flow through me every time I step into my window and see him waiting.

K.

CHAPTER 29

My phone ringing startled me from my reverie, making me drop my pen. I closed my journal and reached for it. After checking the caller ID, I tapped the screen to answer, raising the phone to my ear and said, "Hey, Mom. How are you?"

My dad passed away a few years ago from stage four prostate cancer. Dad had felt like something was wrong for a few weeks before he finally made a doctor's appointment for a scan.

Three months later, he was gone, having refused any treatment. I gave thanks every day that he didn't suffer long.

At first, it seemed my mother might not survive his death. My mom and dad, like Grant and me, were childhood sweethearts and had celebrated their fiftieth anniversary not long before he died. Mom was lost in her grief, and her grandchildren nor I could reach her.

I'd had to move in with her for a few months to help her cope while Grant took care of Jason and Kara. It was a rough time for all of us; my dad had been the rock of our family.

Mom did come out of it, eventually. Now she filled her days with book clubs and yoga for seniors. Now and then, she'd spend a few days at our house, and we'd do routines together down in the basement between lunches and shopping excursions. I tried to call her at least once or twice a week, but now it seemed I had forgotten.

"Well, Katherine, I guess I'm fine, considering my only child hasn't checked on me in nearly two weeks. But enough about me, how are you?"

I withered like a grape in the sun at her tone. I might as well have been a kid again.

She used my full first name when annoyed with me and had done so since I was a small child. It made me as nervous at forty as it did when I was five.

My mother was obsessed with women in history named Katherine. She'd go on and on about Catherine the Great or Katherine of Aragon. She had done her best to raise me to be a strong woman like they had been.

Again, I found myself apologizing for being distant. "I'm sorry, Mom. It's been a hectic few weeks, and Kara's been giving me an extra hard time lately."

I felt slightly guilty for ratting on Kara, but I wasn't lying. She had been more difficult than usual the past few weeks.

As I listened to my mother's voice, I felt tears come to my eyes. I wanted to tell my mom what was going on with me. I yearned for her to fold me in her arms and tell me everything would be all right, the way she had when I was a little girl.

She wouldn't, though. My mother was a practical woman, firm in her beliefs of right and wrong. She'd be more likely to give me a stern lecture which, on second thought, I could use more than a hug.

But just as I didn't want to see judgment on Angie's face if I told her what I'd been doing, I did not want to disappoint my mother. Not one to hold a grudge, my mother had thankfully moved on to tell me all about the new book series she was reading and added that she was sending Jason a sweater she had knitted for him.

It was unlikely he'd wear it, but I wasn't going to tell her that. My mom's knitting skills were, let's just say, less than stellar.

Mom and I planned for her to visit sometime around Christmas. She lived a few hours away and didn't make the trip to see us often. She had never cared much for driving; that had been my father's job.

For the next few minutes, Mom bemoaned missing her grandchildren growing up because we lived so far apart.

I expected this. That was how we finished most of our conversations.

As we ended the call, I leaned on the counter and dropped my head into my hands.

I knew Grant was suspicious of the recent changes in my behavior. I'd let down my mother and my daughter. What was next?

CHAPTER 30

Dear Diary,

This morning I woke up to a violent, noisy thunderstorm. I had the irrational thought that the Gods were angry with me for what I had been doing and were pouring their wrath down upon the earth to let me know of their displeasure.

I stayed in bed much longer than usual, despondent, already sure I wouldn't see him today.

Grant came into the bedroom to see why I wasn't up and moving around yet. When he saw that I was still in bed, he asked what was wrong, so I lied and told him I had a stomach ache. He kissed my forehead and ordered me to rest, and volunteered to take Kara to school today; she couldn't wait for the bus in this weather. Before he left, he offered to bring me some tea and toast, but I couldn't let him do that.

He's such a good man. I don't know that I deserve him anymore.

The adrenaline has somewhat worn off, I think.

Instead of the constant high I felt at the beginning, more and more I feel ashamed of what I'd done. Part of me wants to stop, but the rest of me won't let me.

I understand drug addicts now. It's almost a need, no longer a choice. The highs and lows are also wearing on me, I think.

K.

CHAPTER 31

From the bed, I watched my husband get ready to leave. He works so hard for the kids and me. Meanwhile, I was loafing in bed, in a dark mood because I couldn't dress up and then strip for another man.

I rolled over so I wouldn't have to look at Grant's face and stayed like that until I heard his truck start up. When I was sure he was gone, I climbed out of bed and stretched, shoved my hair into a bun, and pulled on sweatpants.

There would be no exercise for me this morning. I wasn't in the mood.

I felt as gray as the skies outside. I decided I'd lay around and do nothing other than read or nap. Then this evening, I'd do something nice for my family, like make an extra special dinner, or rent a good movie— something to show them how special they were to me.

I also swore I wouldn't go anywhere near the back windows.

Until tomorrow.

CHAPTER 32

Dear Diary,

He showed up. IN THE RAIN!

I couldn't help it. Despite my earlier resolve, I peeked through the blinds, prepared for the disappointment I knew I would feel when he wasn't out there. But he was. He stood in the neighbor's yard, his hair flattened against his head by the rainwater pouring over him. He'd reach up to swipe the water from his eyes, but otherwise, he was still, eyes focused on the window, waiting. Waiting for me.

As soon as I saw him, I held up my finger to tell him to wait for me, and he nodded his understanding, wiping rainwater from his face once more.

I dashed into my closet to find something to put on to please him.

K.

CHAPTER 33

I frantically searched for an outfit, worried he might get tired of standing in the pouring rain waiting for me to get ready.

My fingers found a short, pale yellow, baby-doll-style nightie, and I pulled the tags from it as swiftly as I could. This was another purchase I'd made especially for him, this time online. I wasn't risking another outing where I might run into Stacey or someone else.

On the hanger, it looked sweet and innocent, but when I put it on, the fabric hugged my body like a second skin and was completely see-through. My matching bra and panties showed through the sheer mesh.

I flipped my head over and, upside down, ran my hands roughly through my hair to fluff the curls. I was ready for him. I couldn't wait to see his face when he saw what I'd chosen to wear for him.

CHAPTER 34

Dear Diary,

I grow bolder as days pass, and this goes on.
Today I stood in the window wearing the smallest of bras, a thong that was no more than a scrap of lace, and a pair of spiked heels. I hadn't worn the shoes in years and couldn't come close to being able to walk in them, but I didn't need to.

I didn't even bother with the robe anymore. I situated myself in the center of the window and shoved the curtains to the side, knowing he'd be there waiting. The blinds were already open, so he saw me at once.

I no longer felt embarrassed with him. I turned in a slow circle, allowing him to see the scrap of lace on my butt. It's so strange how just a short while ago, I was mortified that he'd seen me in my sweaty sports bra, and now I was revealing more and more of myself every time I saw him.

I no longer felt old or boring. I felt beautiful and empowered.

He shocked me by reaching down and sliding a hand into the waistband of his cargo pants, but I stayed in place. I couldn't control the blush I felt rising to my cheeks, but I refused to look away. I had learned by then that he always wanted to maintain eye contact with me during our time together. I held his gaze until he finished, and then I closed the curtains with a flourish.

I was a magical creature. I was a sorceress who had cast my spell on him.

In this moment, he was mine.

K.

CHAPTER 35

Dear Diary,

I know I've been absent, but a lot has happened since I wrote last. Something's changed between us. He quickly made it clear that the thong and heels were his favorite outfit, so that's what I had been putting on the last few days. I grew comfortable wearing less and less and displaying my body the way I knew he wanted me to.

But here's where it went wrong. Today, he gestured at his waist and then at me. He had previously used that same gesture to let me know that he wanted me to remove my pants.

Except this time, I wasn't wearing any pants, just the scrap of lace, which barely covered me as it was. As I looked down at him, he made the request again. Finally, I shook my head.

Despite how confident I had gotten in my underwear, there was no way in hell I was stripping naked in my bedroom window. Even I had my limits.

His expression darkened, and he frowned. For the first time since we started this, I saw him mouth words to me. Even though I couldn't hear what he was saying,

I could read his lips, and there was no mistaking his meaning. "Do it now," he instructed me.

I shook my head again, and he surprised me by turning on his heel and angrily stalking off. This stunned me; I'd never seen him look anything other than pleased with me.

Also, I had always been the one to end our "meetings." Confused and a little anxious, I waited a few minutes to see if he'd return. When he didn't, I put on my robe and closed the shades, dejected and sad.

I want to please him, but I don't want to do that. I have my limits. Showing him my most private parts would change everything between us. It would be like turning our story from the one you'd find in a spicy romance novel and turning it into a story on the last page of a porn magazine.

There'd be no mystery, no magic. I'd feel dirty and cheap.

I'm not going to do it. He can take what I offer him or get lost.

K.

~

I tucked my lingerie into a drawer in the back of my closet. Despite the words I'd written, I didn't feel quite that confident. I was aware that this would end at some point, but I wasn't ready. No longer did I try to kid myself that I wasn't hurting anyone. I knew I was.

CHAPTER 36

Dear Diary,

So he stayed away for a week. I can only imagine it was to punish me for denying him what he wanted.

Every morning, I put on one of my outfits and waited. He never showed up, even though I took my regular place every day, hoping he'd come.

Until today.

I was ready in his favorite bra and panties, and when I pushed open the curtains, he was back, and he gave me a long slow nod to show his approval of my outfit choice. He was smiling at me, his earlier anger apparently forgotten, as though last week hadn't happened.

I felt relief flood through me, but it didn't last long. Almost as soon as he spotted me, he began to gesture for me to take my panties off. After my second refusal, he shook his head slowly at me, almost regretfully, and once more, walked away. Again, I waited. Again, he stayed gone.

It was a blessing in a way because minutes later I got the wake-up call it seemed I so desperately needed.

After I had put away my lingerie and dressed in my regular clothes, I went downstairs to start my day.

As I neared the kitchen, I heard my phone buzzing from its charger on the counter. I snatched it up and saw that I had missed three calls from Kara's school and two texts from Kara. I panicked as I listened to the voicemails, imagining the worst.

While I was upstairs, the school nurse had been trying to reach me. She said Kara had been carrying an armload of books and had stumbled over a football someone had left in the hallway.

The irony of that didn't escape me.

Anyway, Kara couldn't see the ball over her stack of books, and she tripped and fell, twisting her ankle. It could have been worse; the nurse thought her foot was probably just sprained, not broken. They had put ice on it and were trying to contact me to come to sign her out. The nurse said I would need to take Kara for an X-ray at our regular family doctor.

The phone call was a cold bucket of water to my face. I had been derelict in my duties as a mother for the last time.

Instead of… whatever I had been doing with the man outside, I should have been available for my daughter when she needed me. I know now that what I have been doing is dangerous and needs to end.

No more. He was gone, and I'd go back to my old life.

It would have been more satisfying if I had been the one to end it with him, but the result is... it's over.

K.

PART TWO – AFTER

CHAPTER 37

Time passes. Memories grow blurry. Facts rearrange themselves in your mind.

Sometimes it felt like I dreamt the whole interlude or read it in some trashy novel I picked up at the secondhand store.

I missed my time with the man outside, but at the same time, I didn't. I didn't miss the stress of waiting each day to see if he'd be there. I didn't miss the anxiety of finding the perfect thing to wear.

And most of all, I didn't miss hiding things from my husband.

It would be more accurate to say that I missed whom I got to be when I was with him. I missed the way I felt about the woman I was in the window.

Proud. Fearless.

After all, it couldn't have been plain old Kat doing those things, acting that way. The bold, confident woman I was in the window was a far cry from my actual self, her personality the polar opposite of mine.

Looking back, I couldn't believe how shameless I'd been with him.

What kind of person shared her body with a stranger, even if no touching was involved? There was no excuse for my actions. I could admit to myself that the adrenaline rush I got from it was as addictive as cocaine.

It was me, Katherine, whom this stunning man wanted to look at over and over, me he would wait for every day. There was a certain power in that.

I made him sweat and clench his jaw over the sight of my nearly naked body. I'd felt desirable and sexy and special for the first time in over twenty years. I didn't feel all those things in my daily role as a wife, mother, and caretaker.

It was no fault of Grant's. I had allowed myself to fall into this routine, this cycle. I should have talked to my husband about how I felt and not looked for something to fill the void I experienced in my daily life.

Regardless, I had to put it, and him, behind me. As thrilling as it had been, I realized how foolish I'd been. I'd risked everything just to feel something again.

CHAPTER 38

Life went back to normal. It was almost as though the interlude never happened.

Almost.

Everything had been peaceful until one Friday evening a few weeks later.

I was in the kitchen prepping dinner, looking forward to a nice quiet meal with my family. Jason was on his way home from college for the weekend, as was his norm, so I was making his favorite spinach and mozzarella lasagna. I couldn't wait to see him and sit with him, Kara, and Grant.

I sipped chilled white wine and hummed a bit to myself while prepping the meal. Grant was already home from work and had gone upstairs to shower and get cleaned up for dinner.

From the kitchen, I heard the front door open, followed by my firstborn's deep voice. I smiled. Everything was better when Jason was home.

Jason was, had always been, a bright ray of sunlight, brightening all of the dark corners of our house.

"Hey, I'm home! Where is everyone?" Jason called from the foyer.

Grinning, I yelled back, "In the kitchen, honey!"

I was holding a bowl of chopped onions and peppers in one hand, and I turned to the sink to rinse the knife I'd been using.

"Hey, Momma, what're you making? Because it sure smells like lasagna!" Jason's deep voice came from behind me.

I turned to face him, still holding the bowl.

Jason threw his arms around me in a bear hug, scooping me up until I was lifted off my feet.

I blushed and playfully swatted the back of his head. "For heaven's sake, son, you'd think we hadn't seen each other in a year."

I was kidding him, and he knew it. Jason was fully aware of how much I looked forward to him coming home on Friday afternoons.

As my feet returned to the ground, I caught a partial glimpse of someone standing behind him.

Jason stepped toward the island, and the person who had followed him into the room came into full view.

I dropped the bowl I'd been holding, scattering vegetables across the tile floor.

It was him, the man from the window, who had seen me mostly naked every day for weeks.

And he was grinning at me with that white, white smile.

"Oops! Butterfingers!" I exclaimed as I quickly sank to my knees and gathered the spilled food.

What the hell?

To buy myself some time, I kept my head down as I said to Jason, "Honey, I didn't know you were bringing someone home with you this weekend?"

Jason made a contrite face as he crouched down to help me clean up the spilled food, sweeping vegetables into a pile with his large hands.

"Oh, yeah, sorry. I forgot to text you earlier. This is my friend, Tyler. Tyler, I'd like you to meet my mother. I hope it's okay I invited him tonight, Mom. I really did mean to let you know before we got here. But it's not like there's not enough food. You know you always make enough to feed an army."

He tossed me a grin that was always guaranteed to melt my heart.

Straightening, Jason dumped the food he'd picked up in the garbage can and then rummaged through some cabinets in search of a pre-dinner snack, unaware of my distress.

Every muscle in my body ached with tension. I could feel knots forming in my neck already.

I was trapped. I couldn't refuse this man a place at my table, couldn't order him out of our home without prompting questions about why I had done so.

My family knew me well enough to know I would never behave so rudely to a guest, even an uninvited, last-minute guest.

I mustered up what I thought would pass for a gracious smile and turned to the man Jason had introduced as Tyler.

It was surreal to find out his name when all those weeks I had just referred to him in my head as "the man" or "he."

I hoped Jason was distracted enough looking for snacks that he wouldn't notice my fake smile or forced tone.

"It's so nice to meet you, Tyler. You are very welcome in our home. My husband and I would be pleased for you to join us for dinner."

I put a little extra emphasis on *husband*, hoping he'd take the hint that Grant was home.

To my ears, my voice sounded brittle and false.

"Thanks for inviting me, Mrs. Browne. I'm sorry to show up on you unannounced like this. Jason told me he'd give you a heads-up before we got here. And you can call me Ty if you'd like. All my friends do. I feel like we already know each other."

Tyler grinned wickedly as he said that. He let the comment hang in the air for a moment and then added, "Jason talks about you all the time."

Behind Jason's turned back, Tyler had the audacity to wink at me.

Furious with his attitude, I glared at him but kept my voice pleasant. "And you can call me Kat. Mrs. Browne is my mother-in-law."

Jason turned toward us, shoveling potato chips from a bag into his mouth. He swallowed and said to Tyler, "Hey, man, let's go put our stuff in my room and get out of my mom's hair. I don't want her to have any excuse to mess up my lasagna."

No way did I want this… person in my house overnight. I tried to mask my dismay. "Oh, um, is Tyler staying over for the night?"

Tyler answered for Jason, his cocky smile in place.

"No, ma'am. I drove my own car. I'm just here for dinner. I've heard so much about your talent in the kitchen, so when Jason invited me, I couldn't pass up the opportunity."

I bet.

Both turned to leave the room, and Jason paused to kiss me on the cheek before heading out of the kitchen and in the direction of the bedrooms, taking the chips with him.

Usually, I'd scold him for taking food to his room, but I couldn't care about that right then. I had no idea how I would get through this dinner.

Tyler paused as he passed me and whispered in my ear, his hot breath brushing the side of my face. "So… it's Kat, huh? I've been wondering what your name is. Kat. I like that. Have you missed me, Kitty Kat?"

With those words, Tyler spun on his heel and followed Jason down the hall.

I felt the hair on my neck rise unpleasantly.

The damn nerve of him.

I collapsed onto the nearest bar stool because I didn't trust my legs to hold me up any longer.

The man was in my house. He had somehow met and formed a friendship with my son. Was this a game he was playing? What would be his next move?

I could only thank heaven that Kara had asked me to spend the weekend at a friend's house. I didn't want my daughter anywhere near Tyler, at least until I figured out what his motives were.

CHAPTER 39

Grant came downstairs shortly afterward, dressed and freshly shaven. A round of introductions was made among the men.

Blissfully unaware, Grant shook Tyler's hand and slapped him on the back, welcoming him into our home as I stood nearby, wringing my hands and smiling nervously.

Finally, we all sat down to eat.

Even though my mind was reeling, I had set the table with my good dishes and stemware, and I'd added a nice bottle of red wine.

I'd have to be careful with how much wine I drank. I wasn't a big drinker; two glasses were usually enough to make me tipsy. I couldn't risk saying something to give myself away.

Dinner was a strange affair. I had to pretend to be pleased to have Tyler as my guest. I tried hard to mask my discomfort, but it wasn't easy. I was worried that at any moment, Tyler would stand up and announce that we already knew each other and how that had happened.

I pushed my food around on the plate, unable to swallow more than a few bites. It all tasted like sandpaper in my mouth.

At least everyone else seemed to be enjoying the meal, especially Tyler, damn him.

He was on his second plateful already, forking up each bite with enthusiasm. Every few minutes, he'd smile across at me and tell me how delicious everything was. Tyler toyed with me and was enjoying it.

Unable to resist any longer, I had to ask the burning question hovering on the tip of my tongue. I couldn't bear not knowing how this man had come to be in my house with my son.

I wet my lips and put on what I hoped was a friendly smile, turned to Jason, and said, "So, tell us, how did you and Tyler meet?"

Jason swallowed his bite of lasagna and wiped his mouth with his napkin before speaking. Even in the middle of this madness, I appreciated my son's fine table manners. I taught him well.

"Okay, so, it's sort of a crazy story," he began, shooting a glance at Tyler. "I was working my shift at the bar a few nights ago, right? It was a pretty slow night, so I was just hanging out, playing a game on my phone, and sipping on a beer between customers."

Catching my look, he said, "Don't look at me like that, Mom. I'm plenty old enough to drink, and my boss doesn't care as long as I don't have more than one or two beers while I'm on shift. So anyway, I started feeling sort of weird and off balance. I got really sweaty, and my vision was kind of blurring in and out like I couldn't focus on anything. The last thing I can remember was trying to make it to a chair, so I wouldn't pass out on the floor. Next thing I know, I'm waking up in the front seat of Tyler's car." He paused to take a sip of his wine before continuing. "Now, I hadn't officially met Ty yet, but he'd been coming into the bar for a few nights before that, and I'd just said hey or whatever when I served his drinks. We didn't talk much other than that. It's hard to make conversation because the music is always so loud in there."

Jason took another sip of wine. Even at his age, it was still strange to watch my little boy drink alcohol.

"So anyway, I came to in his car, still dizzy and kind of freaked out because I had no idea where I was. Ty told me his name and then explained that I had passed out in the bar and he was taking me back to the dorms. He said he had come up to the bar to order another drink and saw me wobbling on my feet. He came over and tried to help me sit, but I collapsed before I could. Ty ended up telling my boss that we were friends and he'd make sure I got home safely."

This is madness.

I struggled to control my expression as I asked Jason, "And did you? Get home safely?"

Jason smiled indulgently at me. "Yes, of course, Mom. Ty got my dorm address and room number from my student ID in my wallet and took me straight there.

He all but carried me inside and helped me get my shoes off, and made sure I drank a bunch of water. Ty ended up sleeping on the sofa in my room. He said he didn't want to leave until he knew I was going to be okay."

What a hero.

I forced myself to smile as I turned to Tyler and said, "Thank you so much for helping Jason. It was really…lucky that you happened to be there right when he got sick."

"It was extremely lucky, and Kat and I are both so grateful you were there," Grant added. "Who knows what could have happened?"

Tyler looked down at his plate, pretending to be embarrassed.

He turned to Grant and said, "It was nothing, Mr. Browne. I'm just glad I was able to help. Jason is a great guy, and I'm really glad we became friends."

Tyler reached a fist across the table and received a knuckle bump from Jason in return.

I felt queasy again and drank some wine to hide my expression.

My jaw ached from how hard I was gritting my teeth.

"Hell yeah!" Jason added with a little too much enthusiasm for my liking. It was clear he had taken to Tyler right away. I struggled to keep quiet.

I didn't believe for a minute that it was a coincidence that Tyler was in the bar where Jason worked. Tyler had to have arranged to meet Jason. But why? And how did he find my son?

A darker thought fought its way forward. Had Tyler somehow purposely gotten Jason sick so that Tyler could come to Jason's rescue? Did Tyler put drugs in Jason's drink while Jason wasn't looking?

And if he had done so, was it all part of some sick plot to get invited into our home?

I left the table as soon as possible, anxious for everyone to finish eating so that Tyler would go. I excused myself to the kitchen, claiming I had a headache and wanted to get a head start on the cleanup.

I needed a minute to think about Jason's story and what it all might mean.

As I rose to leave, Jason offered to help me with the dishes, but I declined. I had to get out of that room, away from Tyler. The very sound of his voice made me sick to my stomach.

I was scraping food from the pots and pans into the trash when two strong arms snaked around my waist from behind. I jumped, then heard Grant's familiar voice in my ear.

My husband gave me a gentle squeeze as he kissed my neck and murmured, "Why so jumpy, sweetheart? You feeling okay?"

I forced my mouth into a bright smile before answering. I turned in the circle of his arms and wrapped my arms around his waist as I tilted my head up to look up at him. "Yes, I'm fine. I think I had a little too much wine with dinner. I'm feeling a bit wobbly. Would you mind carrying in the plates and stuff from the dining room? I'm worried about dropping something. You know these are my good dishes."

Another lie, but I didn't want Grant to see how distressed I truly was by Tyler's presence and the story Jason had told us at the table.

Always happy to help me, Grant returned to the dining room, and I crept to the doorway to listen.

I heard Jason tell Grant that he and Tyler would hang out in Jason's room for a little while. I could hear Grant stacking plates as he told them he and I would be heading to bed shortly.

Grant reminded Jason to make sure the door was locked when Tyler left to go home.

What Grant didn't realize was that the threat was already inside our house.

I wondered where Tyler's home was. Jason might know, but I definitely couldn't ask him. It would be hard to explain why I was interested.

It might have been the wine, but I thought I would have to confront Tyler to find out his reasons for coming.

As Grant rinsed the dishes and I stacked them in the dishwasher, I thought of different ways I could do that.

We worked in companionable silence until the kitchen had been put to rights. I could still hear Tyler and Jason talking in the dining room, but I couldn't make out their words.

I wished they'd hurry up and go to Jason's room, so I wouldn't have to hear Tyler's voice. Better yet, I hoped Tyler would just leave.

When Grant and I went up to our room, he carried a tumbler of whiskey he'd poured to take to bed.

After changing into my nightgown, I was in the bathroom, applying face cream, when Grant came and leaned in the doorway to watch me perform my nightly beauty routine.

I could tell by how his eyes roved over my body in the short nightgown, lingering on my legs, that he'd want to have sex tonight. I was surprised to realize I was eager for it, for him.

I welcomed losing myself in my husband's embrace and craved the security I felt in his arms. After I capped the cream jar, I held my hands out to Grant, pulling him to me.

CHAPTER 40

I wasn't foolish enough to think Tyler would be satisfied with one dinner invitation.

He had a plan; somehow, I just knew that. What exactly that plan entailed, I couldn't say. It was clear, though, that a new game had begun.

There was nothing to be done that day, however. I was dying to grill Jason about Tyler, to ask more questions about the night he and Tyler had met, but I also didn't want to appear too interested. That would raise red flags in a hurry.

It hadn't been the first time Jason had brought a friend home. He collected friends the way other people collected dogs. He was just that kind of person, outgoing and likable, friendly to everyone he met.

Down in the basement, I forced myself through my yoga routine, pushing harder than usual. I had put on my favorite classical music, hoping it would soothe my nerves. However, my heart wasn't in it, and I moved through the poses without paying much attention to my form.

I had gotten into a situation from which I didn't know how to extricate myself. There was no point in wondering what I could have done differently. I already knew the answer. The first time I saw Tyler working on that tree, I should have closed the blinds and gone about my business.

I was a goddamn idiot.

I was almost through with the final poses when I heard the doorbell ring upstairs. I immediately tensed. Wondering who it was and praying it wasn't Tyler, I switched off the music and went upstairs to answer the door.

I peered through the peephole and saw a young blonde woman in a gray uniform standing on my doorstep. She was looking down at a sheet of paper on a clipboard, but I couldn't make out the logo at the top. She appeared to be harmless, so I unlocked the door and opened it a few inches, just enough to let her see my face.

I offered her a polite smile. "Can I help you?" I asked.

She checked her clipboard again. "Are you...Katherine Browne?"

Puzzled, I replied that yes, I was she.

"Fantastic! I'll be right back." She darted down the steps and over to a blue cargo van I hadn't noticed idling at the curb a few houses down.

She reached into the open back door of the vehicle and pulled out a huge bunch of white roses, beautifully arranged with sprigs of baby's breath, in a glass vase.

There had to be at least two dozen flowers in the bouquet. She hefted the vase and started back to the house.

I smiled to myself. Grant. We'd had a wonderful night in bed, me desperate for the reassurance of his touch, him relaxed by the wine and whiskey.

He routinely sent me roses after we'd had such a night together. Judging by the size of this bouquet, I'd outdone myself. The bouquet was so large the delicate white blooms obscured the delivery woman's face..

I relieved the delivery woman of her heavy burden, taking the vase and setting the bouquet on the entry table behind me. The flowers were magnificent, the sweet perfume of the roses already permeating the foyer.

I signed the delivery slip, thanked the woman, and shut the door. I gently touched a white rosebud with a finger, smiling at my husband's thoughtfulness.

Then I noticed something poking out of one side of the bouquet. A tall plastic stick holding a small pink envelope was nearly hidden within the blooms.

I was already mentally writing my thank-you text to Grant as I opened the envelope and pulled the card out. The words were printed in small, neat handwriting.

Thank you for the delicious meal, I hope to see you again soon, T.

He had underlined, "see you again"—the smug bastard.

The Window

I let the card slip from my damp fingers and fall to the floor.

Tyler wasn't done with me, not by far.

Looking more closely at the roses, I only then noticed that the thorns had been left intact on the stems.

CHAPTER 41

After the arrival of the flowers, all was quiet for nearly a week.

I started to relax slightly over the next few days when nothing else happened.

Maybe Tyler had grown bored with this little game and moved on to something more exciting. I could only hope this was the case.

I'd briefly chatted on the phone with Jason the night before, and he hadn't mentioned Tyler at all.

Then the first text message arrived.

I was eating a light lunch of crackers and cheese with fruit and watching a movie in the den, when the phone pinged from the coffee table in front of me. Assuming it was a message from Grant, I set my plate down and leaned over to grab it. I unlocked the screen and clicked the message icon to read the text.

Hey, Kat. Did I happen to leave my glasses there? T.

Angry, I threw my phone down and thought about blocking Tyler's number. Then again, that might make him try to contact me in other ways, so I decided against it. There was no good solution.

It didn't escape me that he could still show up here anytime he chose.

Tyler was screwing with me with this text message. He'd never worn glasses during our encounters, nor was he wearing any when he came to the house with Jason for dinner. I was sure his vision was perfect.

The text was innocent on the surface, seemingly harmless, but I wasn't fooled. Tyler was making his latest move in this game. He was displeased that I hadn't done what he wanted. Instead, I had chosen to end our time together.

I assumed his male pride was hurt. I couldn't imagine he was used to rejection, not with those looks.

I took my time considering if I should reply. After some thought, I decided I should. I worried that if I didn't respond, Tyler would continue texting.

My answer would be a preemptive strike. I typed out and then erased a half dozen replies before settling on a simple **NO**.

I hit the send button and then set my phone to silent mode.

CHAPTER 42

Tyler didn't respond, and a few more days passed with no more flowers or texts.

I wasn't dumb enough to let myself relax this time, though. In my heart, I knew Tyler hadn't gone away for good.

I was driving Kara to school one morning, about a week after the latest text from Tyler. She was telling me about an overnight trip for an out-of-town soccer game she might have to go on, and I could tell by her tone that she was worried I'd forbid her from going.

In truth, getting my daughter out of town for a few days sounded like a great idea. I encouraged her to go and tried to ignore the surprise on her face.

We pulled up to the school drop-off zone, and she got out without a goodbye, as was her norm. I yearned for the days when she'd throw her arms around my neck and beg me not to leave her.

No longer. These days, I was shocked Kara didn't make me drop her off somewhere down the block so she wouldn't be seen with me.

I watched her walk off toward the building, then I pulled my SUV away from the school and turned the car toward home.

There was a pretty little community park about halfway between our house and the school. Sometimes I drove out there and walked on a path that wrapped around the lake, or in nice weather, I just sat on a bench to write in my journal. Sometimes I'd bring crusts of bread to feed the family of ducks that lived in the park.

I'd just decided to turn in for a nice peaceful stroll when I saw a familiar form sitting on a bench at the entrance to the park.

Tyler. He seemed to be staring at me from behind his sunglasses.

When he saw me looking, he sent me a salute before standing and walking briskly away down the sidewalk.

This was too much. Tyler was stalking me. It was no coincidence he'd happened to be sitting at the park where I often liked to spend time.

I considered following him but decided against it, so I continued into the empty lot, found a spot away from other cars, and put my car in park.

I sat for a minute, debating. What should I do? What could I do?

Briefly, I considered telling Grant everything and then going to the police. But how would that make me look? This middle-aged woman exposing herself to a younger man? I'd come off as sad and pathetic.

And Tyler hadn't made any clear threats. He'd sent flowers thanking me for dinner, which was the usual and polite thing to do, and he'd sent me one text message looking for his glasses.

All very innocent, from the outside looking in. It you knew our history, however, it turned into something very different, darker, borderline sinister.

Tyler was being careful. He must have had the same thoughts as I had. He could spin it around on me and tell the police and Grant that I was the one pursuing him, that I had been the one to expose myself to him repeatedly when he was just trying to make a living.

I could see it perfectly in my mind. I'd be humiliated. Tyler could even say he just happened to be at the park that day. It was a public place in a small town. How could I refute his explanation? Even worse, what if Grant believed Tyler's version and not mine?

No, it was better to keep this to myself and see how it played out. Tyler was barely more than a child, playing a childish game. I was the adult, and I'd act like one and deal with him myself.

CHAPTER 43

It soon became clear that Tyler wasn't even finished for the day.

I stopped at the grocery store on the way home to pick up a few things. I intended to try a new, somewhat complicated recipe for dinner. I hoped it would keep my hands and my mind busy.

Grant had been having a rough week at work, also. I thought a nice meal, a few glasses of wine, and a bit of alone time afterward might help ease some of his tension and mine.

I pulled into my driveway and shut off the car. I grabbed my purse and the bag of groceries from the passenger seat, got out of the car, and bumped the door shut with my hip.

I had passed the mail carrier coming down the street, so I went down the driveway to the mailbox and pulled open the door. Tucked in a pile of envelopes was a small white cardboard box about the size of a tape dispenser.

My arms were already full, but I managed to grab the box and the envelopes and stuff it all into the top of the grocery bag.

I let myself into the house and dumped my load onto the kitchen table.

When I took the mail out of the bag, the little white box caught my eye again. I plucked it out and looked closely at it, turning it over in my hands.

There was no address label, nor were there any visible postage marks. Meaning someone had put it in my mailbox.

Just my name, Kat, was written on a black marker on one side of the box.

This time, I knew it wasn't from Grant. I recognized the handwriting. It was the same as the writing on the card that had come with the roses.

I couldn't ignore it, so there was no reason not to open it right then. I took a knife from the butcher's block and sliced the tape holding the box closed. I carefully lifted the lid, holding the box at arm's length, not knowing what I would find.

Inside a nest of white tissue paper was something red and lacy wrapped within the folds. With two fingers, I pulled gently at a scrap of lace.

It was a thong, the same style as the white one I'd worn for Tyler that last day in the window, the one he had made clear was his favorite.

I saw the tiny tag sewn into the back and recognized the brand name. It was one that I knew to be ridiculously expensive, and I'd never bought this brand for myself.

Where had Tyler gotten the money for this?

Or for the flowers, for that matter.

Again, I saw there was a small card tucked inside the box. My fingers shook as I lifted it out.

I flipped it over and read the neatly printed words.

K, they reminded me of your hair. Wear them for me. T.

Tyler had been at my house. Most likely while I was taking Kara to school that morning.

Did this mean he was watching the house? Had he learned my routine and was planning more surprises?

No sooner had I finished this thought, when my phone signaled a new text.

I dreaded reading it. There was no pretending I didn't know who sent it.

I opened the app and read the message.

K, how do you like your gift? I can't wait to see them on you. Just them. Nothing else. Don't you miss it? T.

This time, I was ready. I typed out a response and clicked the send button.

I have no idea what you're talking about.

Don't send me any more gifts, Tyler. I mean it.

CHAPTER 44

Three days later, another small box arrived by courier, addressed to me. I signed for it and took it inside, setting it down on the kitchen table and eyeing it warily.

The box was larger than the first and wrapped in heavy, creamy white paper with a pink bow.

I wanted to throw the box away without opening it. I knew there was nothing good inside, probably more underwear or maybe something even worse.

But no, I had to see what twisted gift he had sent me this time.

When I couldn't stall anymore, I tore the paper off, tossing it aside. I stared down at the box in disbelief. It was a carton of chocolate-covered cherries, the kind you see in every grocery store around Valentine's Day.

Tyler hadn't included a note this time, but his message could not have been clearer.

You had to break through the chocolate outside to get to the sweet cherry center.

I was revolted. My stomach churned as I took the box of candy over to the kitchen sink and dumped the cherries into the garbage disposal. I watched them disappear down the drain, the cherries red as blood.

I smiled grimly, wishing it were that easy to get rid of Tyler.

I crumpled the box and wrapping paper and hid them at the bottom of the trash can where no one would see them.

CHAPTER 45

Tyler was relentless.

This game of cat and mouse went on, crushing my hope that he'd give up and go away if I refused to play with him.

I received more inappropriate gifts in the mail. Sometimes it was nothing more than a card with a suggestive sentence, sometimes expensive underwear.

If I couldn't put whatever it was down the garbage disposal, I burned it in the fireplace.

Once Tyler showed up at the door on a Wednesday and nonchalantly asked if Jason was around. He was aware that Jason was in class on weekdays and only came home on Fridays. It was just a ploy to come around again, to get me shaken up.

I informed him that Jason wasn't home. Tyler tried to get me to let him come in the house under the guise of needing the bathroom before he got back on the highway. When I refused, he just smirked at me and left. I was still determined to wait him out.

Then, the week before Thanksgiving, I got a call from Jason.

"Hey, mom, what are you up to?" he said when I answered the phone.

"Hi, baby. Not much, just sitting here making a grocery list for Thanksgiving. What are you doing?" I asked as I kept writing in my notebook.

Thanksgiving was a big deal in our house; we went all out with decorations, a huge turkey, a ham, and all the trimmings.

"Well, actually." Jason hesitated. "I was calling about Thanksgiving. I was wondering if it was okay if I asked Tyler to come eat with us. He doesn't have family here, and he told me he was just going to get fast food or something. I'd feel crappy if he spent the holiday alone like that."

My heart sank as I told myself I should have expected this phone call. I had to find a way out of this.

"Actually, honey, we're going to go to Gram's this year. You know how much she dislikes driving, especially around holidays. Maybe you can ask Tyler next year, okay?"

I congratulated myself on my quick thinking.

"Oh, okay. I didn't know. I won't mention it to him, then. I have to run, Mom. I have another call coming through. Love you, bye!"

He disconnected the call, and I slumped at the table.

I'd have to rearrange the whole holiday now. My mother had planned to drive to spend Thanksgiving with us, so now I had to spring on her that we'd be going to her house instead.

Grant would have to take a few extra days off, and I knew Kara would hate having to leave her room for days at a time. She loved her Gram, but Kara was most comfortable at home. Not to mention all the questions my family was sure to ask about the sudden change in plans.

Ultimately, it ended up working out fine, despite everyone's surprise.

My mother was glad not to have to make the trip, and for me, it was a relief to be away from home for a few days.

For a little while, at least, it seemed like life was back to normal. I was never truly able to relax, though, wondering what Tyler would be up to when we got back.

Once again, Tyler was messing up my life, but I knew there was no one to blame but myself.

CHAPTER 46

On a Friday evening, Tyler showed up with Jason for dinner again. I was no longer afraid of him. I knew what he wanted. He hoped to bully me into starting our window game again or finishing it the way he wanted me to.

I was not going to do it. I would continue to reject Tyler's attempts.

I had convinced myself that he would eventually give up and go away. Probably.

If he decided to tell Grant or Jason what I'd done in the window, I'd lie through my teeth and deny, deny, deny.

There was no proof, as far as I knew.

The thought crossed my mind sometimes that he might have somehow taken photos or videos of me in the window, but I pushed that idea aside as best I could. I reasoned I'd never seen him with a phone, even though he had one he used to send texts with.

If there were photos, though, I was done for.

I crossed my fingers that there were none.

Resolved instead of surprised this time, I didn't startle when he came through the door with Jason. I knew it had only been a matter of time until Tyler managed to wrangle another invitation to dinner from my son.

I could well imagine Tyler playing the pity card with Jason, crying to Jason that he was all alone in town, playing on my son's soft heart and giving nature.

I had no doubt that Jason would have immediately offered to bring him home for dinner. This was the first time I wished my son would be a little bit less considerate of other people.

When they reached the kitchen, I was ready for Tyler with a smile, and I greeted him in a friendly tone. "Hey, Tyler, nice to see you again. I see Jason forgot to warn me again, but no worries, I made plenty. I hope you like meatloaf."

I continued to slice tomatoes for a salad, my hands steady this time as I worked the knife.

Tyler was quiet behind me. This was such a change from my behavior at the other dinner. I was sure it had him wondering what I was up to. He clearly expected me to be flustered by his presence, but I wasn't giving him that satisfaction anymore.

But I could see Tyler didn't like me turning the tables on him.

He opened his mouth to speak, but before he could say a word, Kara came bounding down the hall into the kitchen. Tyler turned to look at her and put on his most blinding smile.

"And who might this be?' he asked, with a side glance in my direction.

To my irritation, Kara was at once enraptured by him. Tyler was gorgeous and knew his effect on women, apparently including teenagers.

Kara blushed madly and shuffled her feet as she shyly replied, "I'm Kara. I live here. Who are you?"

"Well, hello there, Kara. I'm Tyler, Jason's friend. I'm so sorry I didn't get to meet you last time I was here. May I escort you to the dining room?" He smiled at her, oozing charm from his pores.

I wanted to slap him. Hard.

Kara stammered, "Um... Yes? I mean, yes, thank you, that would be cool." My daughter was bright red to the tips of her ears.

Without a backward glance at me, Tyler held his arm out for Kara to take, and together they left the kitchen.

Oh, hell no. This was not happening.

I rushed to follow them into the dining room. Tyler had already pulled out a chair for Kara at her place at the table and then seated himself next to her.

Keeping my smile was difficult, but I managed to say, "Sorry, Tyler, that seat is reserved for Kara's dad. Why don't you come sit down here on the end?"

"Mom! It's fine. Dad won't care who sits where."

Kara glared at me, murder in her eyes, as only a teenage girl could pull off. There was a challenge in her stare as she silently dared me to insist that Tyler switch seats.

I refused to be drawn into a family argument in front of Tyler, so I said, "Fine, but if Dad wants him to move, he can sit down here."

Point for Tyler.

Thankfully, Jason came in at that moment and took his seat, and the three of them talked among themselves.

Relieved that Kara and Tyler wouldn't be alone together, I left the room, but not before I caught Kara rolling her eyes at me.

We'd have a conversation about her disrespect later. There were bigger issues than her attitude to worry about then.

I returned to the kitchen and opened the oven to check the meatloaf. As I did so, my phone pinged with a text message. I wasted no time reading it.

K, your daughter is stunning, as are you. The two of you look more like sisters than mother and daughter. I am very, VERY pleased to meet her.

I had the uncontrollable urge to take my cast iron skillet into the dining room and bash his head in until his brains spilled all over my grandmother's antique lace tablecloth.

Furious at what he insinuated, I slammed the oven door and angrily tapped out a reply.

Stay away from her, and stop texting me, Tyler. I'm serious.

I kept the phone in my hand a moment longer, assuming he'd reply immediately. When no more messages appeared, I set it down and continued transferring the food into serving dishes.

CHAPTER 47

Kara spent the whole meal eating as little as possible. She hung on Tyler's every word as though he was the most interesting thing she'd ever seen, and anything he said was gospel.

I knew she was of an age where she had a growing interest in boys, but she needed to be looking in any direction except at Tyler. He was not the man she should measure all others against, not the right person for her first crush.

Unaware of the undercurrents, Grant threw me a smile and a wink, enjoying what he thought were harmless schoolgirl antics on her part.

An ache formed in my chest as I watched Kara moon over Tyler. I longed to confide in my husband. Grant and I kept a few secrets from each other, and I felt horrible about keeping one this big. But I knew no good would come out of confessing the whole story to him.

I came up with a plan. I decided I would pull Jason to the side at some point this evening and ask him to please give me a heads up when he was bringing a guest.

Then, if he texted that Tyler would be joining us, I'd cut the meal short somehow, or I'd offer to let Kara spend the night with a friend. I might even be able to fake sickness or a last-minute appointment.

It was my mission, my duty, to keep her away from Tyler as much as possible until this ended; however, it did.

I forced my attention back to the table and saw that my daughter was still making doe eyes at Tyler, and he was doing all he could to encourage it.

I noticed that everyone's plates were mostly empty, so I pushed my chair back as I addressed the table. "Jason, please start clearing the table while I get dessert ready. Kara, go work on your science project. I'll save you some pie for later on."

I knew her project was due Monday, so it was a valid reason to get her to go to her room and away from Tyler.

I also had an ulterior motive. Kara was about to give me another reason to send her to her bedroom.

As I hoped she would, Kara immediately rebelled.

"Mom! I have two freaking days to work on it, and you said we'd do it together on Saturday! Why are you doing this?" Her voice was a screech, and her eyes shot daggers at me.

I felt like an ass because I had told her I'd help her with it later in the weekend. However, this was for her own good.

I snapped back, "I've had about enough of you raising your voice to me, young lady. Now go to your room, and you can forget about dessert. I'll be in later to discuss this."

Kara shoved her chair back so fast that it tipped over and hit the wall, leaving a mark on the paint. She made no move to pick it up as she looked at me in disbelief. I could see the hurt flash across her face, mingled with the embarrassment of being scolded in front of Tyler.

Tears rose in Kara's eyes as she looked right at me and whispered, "I hate you," and ran from the room, swiping at her face with her shirtsleeve as she went.

My heart cracked. Tyler had forced me to hurt and embarrass my daughter.

We all sat there stunned, not knowing what to do.

For once, even Tyler had nothing to say.

Grant was the first to break the awkward silence. "I apologize for my daughter, Tyler. I don't know what's gotten into her."

Always the peacemaker, Jason started to push back his chair, saying to me, "I'll go talk to her, Mom."

I panicked at his offer. I didn't want Jason to leave Tyler alone in there with Grant and me. Now I was going to have to upset, or at least confuse, him too.

I looked at Jason and said sternly, "No, you won't. Leave her be. She needs to be alone to think about her behavior. It's past time for her to learn some respect. You can come help me get dessert ready."

Jason searched my face, looking for hidden meaning in my words. He wasn't stupid and knew me better than most people did. He was fully aware that this wasn't my typical parenting style.

I avoided meeting his eyes and instead looked down at the table. I hated what I had to do and whom I had become to remove this man from our lives.

Jason would forgive me, but I prayed that Tyler wouldn't drive a wedge between myself and Kara. Our relationship was already strained enough.

CHAPTER 48

The next morning, I woke up early. I'd had a restless night, nightmares plaguing me. I dreamt that Tyler was chasing Kara and me through dark woods. I couldn't see her in the gloom, but I could hear her screaming, "Mom, help me!"

In the darkness, I also heard Tyler's dark chuckle as he pursued us both.

I awoke with a start, thankfully cutting the nightmare short. I didn't want to know what happened at the end.

It was a Saturday, but Grant had left an hour or so before to put in a few hours at the office. He was behind on a few of his big projects and sometimes liked going in on Saturday mornings to catch up. Early on weekends, the offices were mostly empty, and he could work undisturbed.

Jason had decided not to stay the night, as he and Tyler headed out to a new nightclub after dinner.

I'd pulled him aside as they got ready to leave. Clutching his jacket sleeve, I begged him to be careful, reminding him always to keep his eye on his drink. I told him that it wasn't only women who had to be cautious of someone dropping something in their glass when they weren't looking.

Plus, I didn't trust Tyler one bit. He'd made it clear he would get to me in any way he could.

This left the house empty but for Kara and me. I lay still, listening for any sound coming from downstairs, but all was quiet. She must still be in bed.

I wasn't looking forward to the confrontation I knew was bound to happen today. I embarrassed her in front of company, and Kara would not be quick to forgive me.

I reasoned that when this was all over, I would do whatever it took to mend our frayed relationship.

I could see it was a bright, sunny morning through the curtains.

Before Tyler, I left the curtains open most nights. I enjoyed watching the stars wink in the dark of the night and waking up to sunbeams playing on my closed lids in the morning.

No more. I felt as though I never wanted to open that window again.

If I could board it up, I probably would. On second thought, no. I wouldn't allow Tyler to take anything else from me.

Thinking I'd surprise Kara with breakfast, I rolled out of bed. Pancakes used to always put her in a good mood.

Yanking on my robe, I headed downstairs to the kitchen. To my surprise, I saw that the door leading to the back patio was partially open.

I peeked out and spotted Kara perched on the edge of one of the pool loungers. She was hunched over her phone, rapidly tapping the screen.

"Kara?" I called her name tentatively as I stepped further onto the patio.

She was startled, then jumped up and quickly shoved her phone into her pocket. "Jesus, Mom, why do you insist on sneaking up on me like that?"

She tried to deflect. The guilt at being caught was written all over her face, and her cheeks were flushed a bright shade of pink.

I ignored her question and accusatory tone and instead asked one of my own. "Kara, who are you talking to this early?"

Again, she rolled her eyes. "No one, jeez. I was looking something up on the internet."

Coming toward me, she brushed past me and into the house, stomping her feet as she went. I fought the urge to snatch her phone and see what she had been doing.

Instead, I let it go, for now, not wanting to fight with her this early, but I had a sinking feeling I knew exactly who she'd been texting.

As I followed her inside, I saw Kara was headed toward her bedroom, so I called her name again to stop her in the hallway.

"Kara? How about helping me make some breakfast? I thought we could have pancakes," I said gently.

I wanted her to stay, to talk about what happened last night. I wanted to wipe the unhappiness from her face, whatever it took. The pancakes were a peace offering.

She didn't turn as she answered. "Yeah, no, I'll pass. I'm not in the mood. I'm going back to bed."

Her bedroom door slammed shut, making my ears ring. She'd made her feelings loud and clear.

I stood in the hallway, trying to decide if I should follow her and force a conversation.

Before I could choose, I heard my phone make the text message sound from upstairs. I jogged up the steps and snatched my phone off its charger on the nightstand. I opened the app and read the short message.

She's so sweet.

I seethed. I knew Kara had been texting Tyler. The fact that she'd been trying to hide it proved that she knew I wouldn't approve.

There were so many reasons this was wrong.

Kara was thirteen. I had no idea how old Tyler was, but assuming he and Jason were of a similar age, he was at least twenty-one.

Any relationship between him and Kara, even a friendly one, was unacceptable.

I'd drive her to and from school and take her phone away before I'd let something develop.

Angie Lee

I knew that Tyler was using my daughter to get to me. He wanted to pick up our game where we'd left off, and he'd use any tactic, including befriending my teenage daughter, to get me to surrender to his will.

CHAPTER 49

Once I grew bolder, so did Tyler. It happened late one night.

The house was quiet and still. Kara had long since gone to bed, and Grant snored softly beside me.

I was sitting in bed, unable to sleep, so I tried to read a novel from the stack at my bedside. My eyes followed the lines of words on the pages, but I wasn't concentrating on what I read and had to start each paragraph multiple times.

I couldn't stop thinking about all that had happened since the first day I saw Tyler behind my house, my decisions, and the damage I'd caused.

Equally consuming was the uncertainty I had about what he'd do next.

Anxious, I'd already chewed my thumbnail down to nothing and was working on my pinky. I thought of going downstairs to get a small glass of whiskey to help me sleep when I heard it.

Plink, plink. A pause. *Plink, plink.*

A light tapping sound on the bedroom window. There were no trees close to the house, so I knew it had to be something else.

I glanced at the bedside clock. Two fifteen in the damn morning.

Carefully pushing the covers aside, I silently slid out of bed. I tugged my robe on and belted it, then padded over to the window. I carefully parted the curtains and looked out into the night.

No longer surprised by anything he did, I didn't react. I just stared down at Tyler. He stood in the yard, backlit by the lights that glowed from the edges of the pool.

When he saw me, he gestured for me to come down and join him.

I shook my head furiously. NO.

He tried again as if he thought I'd come outside in the middle of the night. I didn't care what he had to say. I wasn't doing it.

As I declined once more, I heard Grant speak from the bed behind me.

"Kat? What was that noise? Is someone out there?" he asked, his voice hoarse with sleep.

Shit.

That was all I needed, for Grant to get out of bed and join me at the window.

There was no way I could come up with a good explanation as to why Tyler was in our yard at that time of night, and then what if Grant went out to confront him?

I hurried to reassure him. "It's nothing, honey. Go back to sleep. I'll be right there."

Without sparing Tyler another glance, I drew the curtains shut. Then I took off my robe, climbed back into bed, and curled against Grant's warm back.

Eventually, the sound of his heartbeat lulled me into a fitful sleep.

CHAPTER 50

The next day, yet another package arrived. This one was different from the others. It had no fancy wrapping paper, and no bow—just a large brown envelope.

As usual, my name was written on the package. Again, no postage.

I scooped it up with the other bills and flyers and shut the mailbox.

Once back in the house, I set aside the regular mail and held the brown package in my hand. It felt firm and solid, so I didn't think it was more underwear or candy.

I held it up to my ear and shook it. Nothing.

I took a chef's knife from the butcher block and sliced open the package with more force than necessary, just because it felt good, and then I turned it upside down.

A thick paperback back book slid out of the envelope and onto the counter, facedown.

I flipped it over so I could see the front cover. It was a book I'd never heard of, called The Awakening, and a few more words.

I could see the silhouette of a woman, but the rest of the title and the author's name were hidden by a yellow sticky note in the middle of the cover.

Tyler's handwriting again.

Kat, I think you should read this. Maybe you'll understand me better. T.

No, thank you. I had seen enough.

I decided that any future packages would be left unopened. I gathered the book and the envelope and headed outside to the trash can.

CHAPTER 51

A week later, multiple things happened at once, resulting in the perfect storm.

That morning started relatively normally.

Kara had avoided speaking to me at breakfast, which was no surprise. She was still angry about how I had scolded her in front of Tyler at dinner.

A part of me understood. I was a teenage girl once, and I remember when nothing mattered more than a boy's opinion of me. I kept reassuring myself that I'd make it up to her somehow when all this business with Tyler was finally over.

Hopefully, that would be sooner rather than later. I just had to find a way to make him understand that whatever we'd done in the window, it was over between us. I had no interest in getting back into our game or taking it to the climax that he had deluded himself into believing he was entitled to.

Tyler had seen as much of me as he was ever going to.

I had an appointment scheduled that afternoon with my hair stylist. As each year passed, I had to get my touch-up color done more and more often. I didn't mind sitting in the padded chair and being pampered from head to toe every few weeks. I tried to arrange my manicure and pedicures for the same day as a treat to myself.

Not long after I arrived, I sipped champagne and made small talk with Amber, my regular stylist, as she skillfully unfolded the foils from sections of my hair. After all this time, the two of us were comfortable with each other, and we chatted about a new sushi restaurant that had opened up nearby.

She told me that her cousin, a girl with whom I'd gone to school, had just had triplets through IVF at thirty-eight years old. I couldn't imagine starting over with a baby at this age, much less three, but I was happy for her.

Amber had a daughter about the same age as Kara, so we'd often commiserate on the trials of raising teenagers. Her daughter had been caught sneaking out two weekends in a row, and Amber was at the end of her rope.

I told her about the app we had on our phones, where Grant or I could track the kids' whereabouts and see whom they were texting or talking to and when.

Intrigued, she asked me if the kids minded that we kept tabs on them that way.

I explained that Jason didn't mind. He worked in a club, and anything could happen late at night.

Kara, being thirteen, had no say in the matter. If she wanted to have her own phone, the tracking application was a part of the deal.

Amber thanked me for the advice, saying she would download it for her daughter's phone.

By then, she had finished blow-drying my hair and making loose curls with her flatiron. I closed my eyes, relishing the soothing feeling of her hands in my hair.

From behind me, the door chime announced that someone had come into the salon, and then I heard a voice that filled me with fury.

I turned my head toward the sound, yanking the flatiron from the curl Amber was working on. Pain shot through my scalp, but I tried to ignore it.

It was, of course, Tyler.

He was leaning over the counter, flashing that damn smile at the receptionist, who was already turning into a puddle at his feet.

"Hey there, I was wondering if you take walk-ins? I need a trim pretty badly."

The poor girl stuttered. "Um... I... I can check if we can fit you in."

Tyler turned his head and looked directly at me as he drawled, "Yes, please fit me in."

I'd had enough.

I jumped from the chair and stalked over to him, leaving Amber openmouthed behind me, with the flatiron frozen in her hand.

I grabbed Tyler by the wrist and said in a low voice, "Can I talk to you? Outside?"

It wasn't a question. I was already dragging him out the door. Once outside on the sidewalk, I let go of his arm as though I'd been burned.

Not so long ago, I'd dreamed of the feel of his skin, but now, touching him, I felt nothing but disgust and anger.

Above our heads, thunder rumbled as I faced him.

"What the hell, Tyler? Why are you following me? This is... too much. What do you want from me?"

I knew the people inside the salon were watching us through the window, but I didn't care at that moment. I'd find a new salon if I had to. I just wanted Tyler out of my life.

"I don't know what you mean, Kitty Kat. I just stopped in to get a haircut, same as you. It looks great, by the way." His voice was laced with sarcasm, and I wanted to strangle him.

I took a deep, calming breath as I considered a different approach. Anger wasn't getting me anywhere with him. I'd try to appeal to his ego instead. I knew he had one, and it was massive.

In a softer tone, which I usually reserved to get my kids to agree to something, I said to him, "Tyler. Please stop all this. The visits, the gifts, all of it. This is borderline stalking. You have to know that it's over between us. Yes, I enjoyed the time we spent in the window, but that's finished now. You want more than I can give you. Can't you please let this go and leave me and my family alone?"

He paused before speaking. I could see him turning my words over in his mind.

"Kat, look. What we did... it ends when you take off all your clothes for me. That's all I want. You led me to believe that's what I'd get in the end, and then you denied me. You're the worst kind of tease. Now that I think about it, I'm the one who should be angry here."

He crossed his arms and glared at me. I couldn't believe the audacity of this man. Tyler was gaslighting me, trying to convince me that I had wronged him somehow.

The clouds broke, and it started to sprinkle. I looked up at the sky, took another deep breath, and changed tactics again. Playing nice was not going to work.

"If you don't leave us alone, I'll go to the police and get a restraining order. I'll tell them you've been stalking me."

Tyler laughed at me, but his smile turned ugly.

"No, I don't think you will. I'm not stupid, Kat. You have no proof other than a few harmless little text messages. If you go to the police, I'll sit down with Grant and tell him all about what you've been doing in your bedroom window while he works his ass off all day. Then I'll drop in on Jason and let him know what his beloved mother has been up to. How do you think he would feel, huh? Just imagine how disappointed in you your precious son would be. So, you see, it would be much more beneficial for both of us if you'd just give me what you owe me."

The sprinkle became a downpour, and I realized he was right.

I didn't ever want Jason or Grant, or anyone, to know what I'd done.

The power this man had over my life was nauseating.

The police would ridicule or dismiss me. My son would never look at me the same, and Grant... who knew what Grant would do? What if he left me?

Unable to look at Tyler anymore, I spun on my heel and went back inside the salon.

CHAPTER 52

Once inside, I apologized to Amber for running out as I dug my credit card from my wallet to pay her. I was shaking so hard, my hands fumbled with my purse, and I nearly dropped the card.

I could see Amber was dying to ask me who that man was, but thankfully, she restrained herself. My freshly done hair was now in ruins, so I pulled it back into a ponytail as I waited for a receipt.

She noticed and offered to fix it. "Kat, we could dry it again, and start over with the iron, if you want?"

Amber's voice was eager as she made the offer. I knew she wanted me back in her chair, captive, so she could grill me about what had happened outside.

I smiled wearily at her and shook my head. "Thanks, Amber, but I think I'm just going to head home. I'll call you in a few weeks for my next appointment, okay?"

Amber's disappointment was obvious, but she let it go.

After leaving her a generous tip, more than twice the usual amount, I left the salon and headed home.

On the way, I stopped at the liquor store and slowly browsed the aisles. I knew I'd need some liquid fortification this evening, and our bar cart was low on wine.

After selecting two reds and a white, I added a bottle of Grant's favorite bourbon whiskey. Once Grant had a few drinks, there was no chance he'd notice how upset I was. Alcohol would minimize that risk.

I had no idea my day could get any worse until it did.

I was almost home, driving down our street when I saw it.

Tyler's car was parked along the street, almost in front of our house. I hit the gas and turned into our driveway.

There, on my front porch, were Tyler and Kara sitting in the swing together.

I could see Kara laughing at something he said as I sat in my car in the pouring rain, staring in disbelief at the two of them.

I glanced down at the clock, shocked at the time. I didn't realize how long I'd been in the liquor store, and now Kara was home from school.

Home alone. Alone with Tyler.

I got out of the car and stalked toward the porch, oblivious to the rain pouring over my head and down my body.

"Kara! What the hell are you doing?" I shouted at her, not caring that I'd raised my voice at her again. "Get in the house right now!"

"Mom! I wasn't doing anything. We were just talking!"

She flinched at my tone as she stood up from the swing, but she didn't make any move to go inside. Instead, she stood her ground, arms crossed over her chest defiantly.

"Kara. I said, now! Go!" I jabbed a finger toward the front door.

Finally, Kara ran inside, blinking back tears.

I turned on Tyler, furious. He had lazily flopped in the porch swing, one arm thrown insolently across the back.

"Long time no see, Kat."

Looking at his smug face, something in me broke.

I couldn't take another confrontation today. I was bone weary and didn't have it in me.

Letting him take another point, I rubbed my eyes with the heels of my hands and replied, my tone defeated, "Just go home, Tyler."

I didn't bother waiting for him to respond. I walked inside and closed the door behind me, locking it.

Later, after some wine, I was somewhat calmer, so I composed a text message to him.

I don't want you at my house and I don't want you near my daughter. Please stay away from us.

I received his reply almost immediately.

You know how you can make that happen.

Resisting the urge to throw it, I set my phone on the table and walked down the hall to Kara's room.

I dreaded this. In her eyes, I was the bad guy, a monster. I prayed that one day she'd understand that I had done all of this to protect her from the real threat.

I knocked softly on Kara's door and called her name. "Kara? Can I come in?"

I heard her muffled voice from inside. "I don't care."

That was as close to permission as I was going to get, so I turned the knob and entered.

Kara's room was a dark cave of bad music, black clothes, and teen angst. The walls were covered with her drawings, her poetry, and pages torn from books. For some reason, she liked to circle her favorite passages and hang them on the walls. I left it alone because I felt it was preferable to her writing on the walls.

I could see a small lump in the bed under the dark purple velvet comforter that I knew was Kara.

Her sniffles reached me in the doorway, and the sound tugged on my heartstrings.

She'd been crying.

I stepped further into the room, closing the door behind me. I walked to the bed and sat on the edge, placing my hand tentatively on the lump where I hoped Kara's head was.

"Kara, I know I embarrassed you in front of Tyler, and I'm sorry for it," I began. "I don't expect you to understand this right now, but please trust me when I tell you he isn't someone you need to be hanging out with." I paused, trying to decide how much to reveal. "There are many reasons, but the biggest is that he's too old for you. He's at least ten years older than you. I love you, and I don't want you to get hurt by having a crush on a much older guy."

This wasn't the whole truth, but I hoped it would be enough.

Kara shoved the covers off and sat up. Her eyes were puffy and red from the tears she'd cried, and I ached to take her in my arms.

I knew it wouldn't be welcomed, so I sat there, helpless to do anything to comfort her.

She was so, so young. In her swollen face, I could still see the sweet, affectionate toddler she had been not that very long ago.

"Mom, just listen to me, okay? We were just talking. Nothing else. Tyler was driving by as I was getting off the bus, and he saw me and stopped to talk for a minute. I'm not an idiot. I knew you wouldn't want me to let him in the house, so we stayed outside on the porch. It was perfectly fine. I mean, it wasn't like he was going to do anything to me. He's not some stranger. He's Jason's friend! It's like... I hate when you treat me like a baby like I can't make good decisions or something."

This was the most words she'd said to me at once in a long time, years maybe.

A part of me understood where she was coming from, but that didn't change anything. I didn't want Tyler within a hundred yards of her.

Resigned that I couldn't change or fix anything with Kara right then, I patted her knee and left her room.

CHAPTER 53

Two days later, Tyler paid me a visit at home.

It was midday, and I was puttering around in the backyard after skimming the pool for leaves.

I was tempted to take a soak in the hot tub. My neck muscles were rock hard with tension from the last few weeks, and I thought the hot water would be soothing. I could grab some wine and a book from the house and spend the next hour relaxing in the jets.

I was headed back inside to change into my swimsuit when I noticed that my herb pots on the patio were a bit dry and could use a little water. Changing course, I went around the side of the house to get the water hose.

I turned the corner and gasped.

Tyler was standing at the gate to the backyard, grinning at me.

"Hey, Kat. We need to talk, don't you think?"

I felt ill. I should have been more vigilant and should have known he would show up here.

He had me trapped in my yard. Sickened but trying my best to appear confident, I stood my ground and faced him.

Coldly, I demanded, "What now, Tyler? Say what you came to say, and then leave me and my family the hell alone."

He smiled. I couldn't believe that once I thought his smile was so beautiful, so charming. Now I could see the manipulator hidden behind that distracting exterior.

"I just want to see you, Kat. I won't touch you. I promise. Listen… I'm what people in certain circles call a voyeur. It's my kink. I get off just from looking at women's bodies in lingerie and watching them undress for me. Anything beyond that is of no interest to me."

He shrugged, like what he'd described was no big deal.

I frowned. I'd never heard of such a thing, but there was a ring of truth to his words. He hadn't ever tried to touch me or even let on that he wanted to.

I kept quiet and waited, knowing he had more to say.

Tyler went on. "You teased me for weeks, made me think you were working up to baring it all. If you agree to finish where you left off, I'll leave you alone after you do it. Just… give me what I want, and this will be over. If you don't agree, I'll tell Grant and Jason everything. If that doesn't work, well let's just say Kara is the spitting image of her mother. And I think she really likes me."

I flinched at his last words and prayed he hadn't seen my reaction. His thinly veiled threat set my blood to boiling and rage clouded my vision.

How dare he threaten my daughter!

The urge to wrap my hands around his neck and squeeze until he was dead was a primal need burning through my veins.

Of course, I couldn't do that. Tyler outweighed me by at least a hundred pounds, and besides, he held all the cards here.

I was no longer powerful, no longer in charge. Tyler had me right where he wanted me, backed into a corner, and we both knew it.

It was no longer possible for me to come clean with Grant; confessing wouldn't keep Tyler away from my daughter. Also, even though Grant was easygoing most of the time, I knew that faced with someone threatening Kara, Grant would react violently. I couldn't risk something happening to Grant if he got into an altercation with Tyler.

I was on my own. Unable to hide the disgust from my expression, I looked at him and said, "Give me a second to think."

I turned my back on him and paced the yard. I was devastated that Tyler would involve Kara to get his way, but I couldn't take the chance that it was an idle threat. She looked at Tyler with hero worship and had more than a little crush on him.

I'd seen her staring dreamily at him over the table when Jason had brought him to the house for dinner and again when they were on the porch.

If Jason came home for the weekend and didn't bring Tyler, Kara was the first to ask why he wasn't there. Her disappointment was clear in the slump of her shoulders when she realized Jason had come alone.

Could I do it? Could I disrobe for this madman to save my family and get my old life back?

He had promised there would be no touching. I tried to rationalize the idea. It would barely be more than I had already done for him; just two more scraps of cloth, and it would be over.

I had to admit to myself that there wasn't much choice. I had to protect my daughter at all costs.

CHAPTER 54

The only possible answer was, yes, I could do it. I had to.

It was clear he wouldn't let me out of his game without this final humiliation. I would give Tyler what he wanted and hope he would uphold his end of the bargain. If he didn't, I would come clean to Grant and damn the consequences, whatever they were. Either way, I'd have control of my life back.

I turned to face Tyler and said with a raspy voice, "Yes."

I cleared my throat and then repeated, in a more confident tone, "Yes, I'll do it."

Tyler's eyes widened with surprise. He'd been playing with me all along, not truly expecting me to agree to his terms. I could see him considering my sudden change of heart, and I knew he was wondering if I was being straight with him.

"Tyler, I want my life back. I want you gone, and I want to forget you ever existed. If this is what it takes, I'll give you what you want. We started this together, and we will end this together. Come to the house tomorrow morning at eleven. Just don't come to the front door. Park down the block and come through this back gate, and wait right here. When you see me in the window, that will be your signal to come in the back door. I'll be waiting, and we'll finish this. And you leave your phone in your car, do you understand? I'm not risking you trying to take any photos. Do we have a deal?"

Tyler's brow furrowed, and he narrowed his eyes at me, analyzing my words and still trying to find the catch. I knew he imagined all the ways this could go.

I hurried to speak again, reassuring him that my agreement was genuine. I was afraid he'd have second thoughts and call the deal off.

Again, I tried to play to his ego. "Tyler, you are in charge here. What choice do I have but to agree? Come to the house, as I said. I'll be ready, just the way you want me. This isn't some kind of trick, okay?"

For a moment, I was sure he was going to argue.

Finally, his face cleared, and his lips twisted in a half-smile. He seemed satisfied as he said, "Okay, Kitty Kat. But we're going to finish this in your bedroom, where it all started. I'll see you tomorrow. All of you."

With those words, he turned and walked back the way he came.

Fighting the urge to vomit, I followed him, slamming the gate behind him and locking the latch.

I leaned against the smooth wood and closed my eyes, lightheaded from the confrontation and the anxiety of being alone with him.

Yes, I can do this. I must.

Even though the thought of being naked in front of Tyler made me physically ill, I could do it to save my family.

CHAPTER 55

I didn't sleep at all that night. Instead, I lay tossing and turning next to Grant, envying him his deep slumber.

Looking at his face, peaceful in sleep, I knew I had to go through with my arrangement with Tyler. I had made the choices that led me to this. In my selfishness, I'd begun something I never should have, and it was up to me to finish it.

I'd been blind to my charmed life, ungrateful for all I'd been blessed with.

I deserved no less than the humiliation of stripping against my will for Tyler.

Tomorrow would be the punishment for my sins.

CHAPTER 56

The next day started like any other day, but I knew it would be anything but routine.

Grant left on time for work, oblivious to my torment, kissing me as he walked out the door and down the driveway to his car.

Everything in me wanted to reach out and pull him back to me, to confess everything and beg for his understanding.

I didn't.

I just watched from the doorway as he drove away.

I hoped cleaning up this mess wouldn't take long, and I could finally get my life back.

The minute they were safely out of the house, I went upstairs to prepare.

I showered until the hot water ran cold, as though I could burn away all thoughts of what I was about to do. I washed my hair and shaved every inch of my body that would be exposed.

After drying my hair, I used the flat iron to arrange it into soft curls. I applied scented lotion to every inch of my skin but left my face bare.

Tyler had never seen me with makeup on, so there was no reason to use any today. Besides, it wasn't my face he was coming here to see.

Nausea threatened again. I pushed it back, focusing on my preparations.

In the closet, I found his favorite lace bra, the white thong, and those goddamn spike heels.

I hated the sight of them. They were symbols of how I had let my family down, even if they weren't aware of it. I wavered in my decision for a split second, but then I called up the face of my little girl to help strengthen my resolve.

I was going the distance with this, whatever it took to get him out of our lives.

Looking in the full-length mirror, I critically checked each exposed inch of my body for imperfections and found my reflection more than acceptable.

Even though I no longer cared about Tyler's opinion of my body, I needed him to be satisfied. He had to feel as though he had won this final phase of the game. Making his dream come true was the only way it would work, so there was no chance in hell I would give him the opportunity to claim I hadn't held up my end of the deal.

At a few minutes to eleven, I readied myself in my bedroom. I mentally reminded myself of all the reasons I needed to do this and tried to stay calm.

It wouldn't do me any good to be a nervous mess when Tyler arrived. I knew enough about him to know that he wanted me standing tall and proud, with nothing on but my underwear and my confidence.

At precisely eleven o'clock, I untied my robe and let it slide to the floor.

Wearing just underwear and heels, I stepped into the window.

As I knew he would be, Tyler was standing in the backyard, waiting. His eyes were trained on the window, and even from this distance, I could see the tension in his neck and shoulders.

I imagined he was also worried that I'd back out at the last minute.

His mouth rose in a half-smile as he gave me a sarcastic salute and then disappeared from my view, presumably headed to the back door as I'd told him to.

I started to close the curtains but decided not to. This would be over soon, and it might make him happy to see them open.

There was no turning back now.

Mere seconds later, I heard the back door open and then shut, hinges creaking. Then his footsteps as he walked slowly across the wood floors.

Finally, Tyler appeared at the bottom of the stairs and bent his neck to look up for me. He spotted me standing there, nearly naked.

Even from the second floor, I could see his pupils dilate. He put a steadying hand on the newel post but didn't speak. His eyes roved the length of my body, from my red curls to my painted toenails in the heels.

Still silent, he made his customary gesture, rotating his forefinger, which meant he wanted me to spin around for him.

I was afraid I'd trip and fall in the high heels, so I made a slow, careful circle, allowing him to look his fill, and then he motioned to me to make a second turn.

After a few moments passed, he pointed to my bra and finally spoke to me, his voice low and rough. "Your bra. Take it off. Do it slowly."

I hesitated, and then once more, I forced Kara's face to my mind and held it there like a talisman, giving me the strength to do what I must.

Never breaking eye contact, I reached around my back to unhook the clasp of my bra. Luckily, it went smoothly, without catching.

I had to play out my part perfectly, doing everything exactly as he'd envisioned if I had any hope of escaping this unbearable situation.

The thin straps slid off my shoulders, and my bra fell to the floor.

I stood still, only slightly trembling, as Tyler drank his fill of my naked chest.

I was mortified at my nakedness and had to force myself not to lift my hands to cover myself.

But that wasn't how we played the game, and he would not be pleased with me if I denied him this pleasure.

By this time, Tyler was almost panting with desire, and, unlike me, he wasn't ashamed of it. He did nothing to hide his very clear reaction.

He spoke again. "Now, the rest. But, Kat? Leave the shoes on. You know how much I love them."

Sick bastard.

Despite the warmth of the room, I felt chilled, and goosebumps rose on my arms, legs, and chest.

I was revolted by him, and by myself, and by what I was doing.

Every bone in my body rebelled against what he wanted me to do, but I had to see this through to the end.

For Kara. For Grant and Jason. And for me.

I gazed down at him and asked, in a strong, clear voice, "If I do this, we're done, right? I'll never see you again, and neither will any of my family."

Tyler's attention was so focused on my chest I wasn't sure he was even listening, but then he replied impatiently, "Yes, Kat, I told you this is all I wanted from the beginning. Don't ruin this for me. I want you to take your panties off. You'll do it for me and make it good, or I'll make you touch yourself, too. Now, I'm coming up. I told you I wanted this to end in your bedroom."

He slowly climbed the stairs, wanting to draw this last scene out to prolong his pleasure, his eyes never connecting with mine.

I was no longer a person to him. I was just an object, a toy. I didn't care. It was almost over.

I backed up two steps to give him room on the landing.

You've got this, Kat, I told myself.

As Tyler lifted his foot to climb the last step, I rushed forward, planted my hands on his broad chest, and shoved him as hard as I could, putting all my body weight behind the push.

His mouth formed an "O" of surprise as he tumbled backward down the stairs, his feet flying over his head as he fell.

His heavy body crashed to a stop as he landed in a heap on the floor.

CHAPTER 57

People say that what doesn't kill you only makes you stronger. I disagree.

What doesn't kill you comes back and tries again.

Tyler would never have gone away and left me alone for good. He would have continued to stalk and terrorize my family and me for who knows how long.

He might have followed through on his subtle threats about Kara. That was a risk I was not willing to take.

Tyler had to die. There was no other choice.

I was going to kill him, and it had to look like an accident.

I had been plotting how to get rid of him for days, making one plan, discarding it, and starting over. Yesterday's visit gave me the perfect idea.

I had considered poison, but there would be a risk of Grant or one of the kids getting the wrong dinner plate. I thought about running him over with my car, but then I'd have to hide the damage somehow until I could have it repaired.

How would I pay for that when Grant and I had joint credit card accounts?

Finally, I decided luring him to my house under the guise of surrender would be the only thing that would work.

If I seemed nervous when he got there, well, that was to be expected, considering what he'd thought I was going to do for him.

And so far, my plot had gone off without a hitch.

At least, it appeared as if it had.

Time to put part two of my plan into motion.

Tyler lay still at the bottom of the stairs, staring sightlessly up at me. A thin stream of blood trickled from one of his ears.

From upstairs, I could see his spine bent at an unnatural angle. I was pretty sure his neck was broken, but I needed to be one hundred percent certain he was dead.

I kicked off the damn heels I so despised and crept carefully down the steps, stopping halfway down.

"Tyler?" I called his name tentatively, once, then again.

"Tyler, are you all right?"

I madly giggled at my joke. Tyler was clearly not all right.

Nothing.

I watched him for a full five minutes, looking for a blink, a twitch, or any sign of life. His chest didn't appear to move, so I didn't think he was breathing.

Finally, I was satisfied. No one's body could be twisted like that, and they be able to hold back a cry, a whimper, or some physical reaction. It was impossible.

Tyler was dead. Good riddance.

This was far from over, though. The real work was only beginning.

I had to set the stage now, and this was the most crucial part of my plot.

There could be no question as to what had happened here. It all had to be perfectly executed if I had any intention of getting away with murder, and I certainly did intend to do so.

Prison jumpsuit orange would not look good with my hair.

I ran quickly back upstairs to my bedroom, scooping up my bra and shoes as I went. I dashed into my closet and stashed the bra and shoes in a rarely used bottom drawer filled with heavy winter sweaters I never wore.

I'd come back and dispose of them later.

A small stack of folded clothes waited at the end of the bed. I hurriedly dragged on the t-shirt and leggings, clothes I'd wear on a typical day at home.

I ran my hands through my hair to loosen the curls I had so painstakingly created earlier, then took a tie and quickly wrapped my hair into my customary bun.

Wait. That wouldn't do. It was too neat.

I pulled pieces of hair out here and there to make it look tousled and wild, as though I'd been in a fight.

When I was satisfied with my disheveled appearance, I paused and looked around the room.

What else needed to be done? I consulted my mental checklist for my next step.

Moving to the bed, I pushed my bedside lamp onto the floor, wincing as the porcelain base cracked. It sent a noise like a gunshot through the quiet room.

I yanked the comforter halfway off the bed, allowing the end to drape on the floor, and then surveyed my handiwork with a critical eye.

Now it looked like a struggle had taken place in the room.

I paused for a moment but heard no noises coming from downstairs.

Reassured by the silence, I continued my work.

I took the top of my t-shirt in both hands and yanked, ripping the neckline and tearing one of the shoulders nearly off.

I dreaded what I had to do next, but it had to be done. I went to the door leading to the bathroom and braced my hands on the frame. I took one deep breath and then slammed the side of my face into the wooden doorframe.

I let out a cry that could wake the dead, although I sincerely hoped it wouldn't.

Pain radiated through my face, and I let the tears flow, hoping I hadn't fractured my cheekbone, but I knew an injury would lend credibility to the story I would have to tell soon.

I looked at the evidence I had just created. A bloody smear shone wetly on the white wood of the doorframe.

Perfect.

Satisfied, I peeked in the mirror over the dresser to assess the damage. I had split the skin of my cheek, and my face was already covered in blood.

Excellent.

Things were going according to plan. The stage was set.

I crossed back to the stairs and peered down at Tyler's body. As far as I could tell, he remained in the same position he had landed in.

I descended slowly and kept my eyes locked on his, double-checking for movement. When I reached the bottom step, I hopped over his broken body.

The blood was still running from his ear and forming a ghastly puddle on my floor.

I frowned in disgust. That would probably leave a stain.

I looked around one last time to make sure everything was in place to back up my story.

Tyler had attacked me, *check.*

We struggled, *check.*

I ran down the stairs, and he chased me, stumbling and falling to his death.

Check.

Taking a deep breath, I went to the front door and reached for the knob.

It was showtime.

CHAPTER 58

I opened the door and fell out onto the front porch, leaving it open behind me. I allowed my knees to buckle just in case anyone was watching, and I sat in a jumble, screaming as loudly as I could.

"Help me, help me! Oh my God, somebody, please help me!"

Forcing myself to sob, I kept shrieking for help.

It wasn't that difficult to get the tears to flow. My cheekbone did feel broken and was throbbing angrily, pounding in tune with my racing heart.

I prayed that someone would hear my pleas soon and come to the rescue.

James, our neighbor from two houses down, happened to be walking his Labrador retriever, Jake— my timing was impeccable.

As he neared the house, James whipped his head toward my voice.

James dropped Jake's leash and ordered Jake to "stay" before he sprinted across my yard.

Wagging his tail, Jake planted his butt on the sidewalk to watch the show.

Good dog.

"Jesus, Kat, what the hell happened to you? Did you fall down the stairs or something?" James asked, climbing the steps and dropping to his knees to crouch next to me on the floor.

I saw his shock as he took in my torn clothes and the blood dripping down my face.

James hurried to reach into his shirt pocket, where I assumed he had his cell phone.

I sobbed harder and louder, forcing a few words out here and there, and clutched his shirt for dramatic effect. "He... he... inside... fell... call police."

More sobs. "Call Grant. Please help me."

I clung to James for the full effect as I continued churning out the tears and sobs. I thought I was doing a pretty good job of being convincing.

It was a stroke of luck that James had heard me and come to the rescue.

He was a big teddy bear of a man, soft-hearted and always offering to help his neighbors with this or that chore. Over the years, he'd come over many times to carry my groceries in from the car.

I couldn't have chosen a better knight in shining armor. This was going much better than I'd hoped or expected.

It couldn't have been more than two minutes later that James was connected to emergency services. He hurriedly recited our street name and my house number and pleaded with them to hurry, telling the dispatcher that his neighbor had been attacked and was badly hurt and bleeding.

Again, he told them to come quickly and ended the call.

James pulled napkins from his fanny pack and awkwardly tried to blot the blood from my face.

My cheek screamed in agony with every touch of the rough paper. I didn't mind; the pain made it easier to force the tears.

James made soothing noises as he held me, slowly rocking me back and forth as if I was a small child as I continued to cry silently in his arms. I'd stopped openly sobbing by this time, not wanting to take the act too far.

He asked no further questions and let me soak his shirt with my tears and blood.

Mere minutes later, two black and white police cars, sirens blaring, came to a screeching halt in front of my house. One car parked in the driveway, and the other stopped sideways in the street.

Three navy-uniformed police officers burst from the two vehicles, each resting their hands on their guns at their hips. As the officers came closer, I heard chatter from their radio speakers.

One officer spoke into his shoulder using coded language I didn't understand. I assumed he was letting the dispatcher know they had arrived on the scene, or maybe he was describing what he saw.

Hysterical woman being comforted by a large man wearing a fanny pack.

The Window

Witnesses: One dog.

Over and out.

The first officer to reach the porch steps was a female. She climbed up and then crouched to look at me as the other two officers, both men, waited on the lawn for orders.

She shot a glance at James and said, "Please step back, sir, and let me have a look at her." She gave him a reassuring smile to soften her words.

James at once stood and backed away but continued to hover nearby.

The lady officer looked at my face and grimaced at the mess I'd made of my cheekbone. She spoke to me so gently as though she was afraid I'd break.

"Ma'am, I'm Officer Anne Dixon, and we're going to help you, okay? Can you tell me your name and a little bit about what happened here?"

Here we go. I had to make this good.

My future, and that of my family, depended on my actions during the next few hours.

When I felt the tears were in danger of drying up, I'd envision myself handcuffed, being shoved into the back of a police car, and headed to the police station to be charged with murder.

That definitely got the waterworks flowing again.

I started with a small sob for good measure, then wiped my nose on the bottom hem of my ruined shirt before responding.

I spoke haltingly, a word or two between sniffles. I kept my eyes downcast as I mumbled my name. "I'm Kat." Sniff.

"I mean… my name is Katherine Browne. He… he attacked me. Tyler… attacked me." Sob.

"My son's…my son's friend. He's… still inside."

That got her attention.

Alarmed, Officer Dixon shot to her feet. She waved urgently to one of the other officers and gestured with her head for him to go into the house.

Then she turned to me again. "Okay, Kat, can you try to stand up for me? I'd like to move you off the porch and away from the house. Is that okay?"

Turning to James, she added, "Sir, thank you for staying with her. You can go wait down on the sidewalk now, but please don't leave the area. An officer will be coming soon to take your statement."

Eyes wide at the situation he'd found himself in, James nodded, his chest puffed out with self-importance. "Yes, ma'am. Will do."

I was surprised he didn't salute her.

Now that the police had arrived, I think James was excited to be a part of the drama unfolding in our usually quiet neighborhood.

James walked off the porch and down the steps to the sidewalk. Jake was still sitting in his place on the concrete, dutifully waiting for his master. James bent and picked up Jake's leash where he'd dropped it, and together they continued to watch the show.

I had the sudden irrational thought that perhaps someone should bring the two of them some popcorn, and I had to stifle a giggle.

Laughing at this point would be highly inappropriate and likely arouse suspicion.

On the other hand, maybe I was hysterical, which was why this act came so easily to me.

After all, I had just killed an unarmed man.

That is a valid reason for anyone to fall apart, I thought.

One of the male officers climbed the porch steps and approached the partially open door with his gun drawn.

Officer Dixon gently took my elbow and helped me rise to my feet. "Okay, Kat, easy now. Take your time."

Together, she and I walked down the steps as she signaled to the third officer.

He must have known what she wanted because he rushed to open the back door of one of the patrol cars, and she carefully guided me to sit.

"Just sit here a little while, Kat. Will you be okay if I leave you on your own for a few minutes?" she asked. "Officer Gale here will keep an eye on you. Let him know if you need anything."

She turned to whom I presumed was Officer Gale and commanded, "Get her some water and an ice pack, Dan. And make damn sure you write down anything she says, no matter what it is, got it?"

Officer Gale nodded, clearly used to deferring to her.

It was just another stroke of luck for me to have a female officer in charge. I figured a woman would likely be much more sympathetic about my "assault."

I didn't much care for being stuck in the backseat of this police car, though.

I looked warily at the wire mesh screen separating me from the front and hoped this was the only chance I'd get to sit there.

Officer Dixon strode back to the house and paused at the door to speak with the officer who had gone inside. I hated that I couldn't hear what they were saying.

The male officer stood in the doorway, his face grim. He gestured to Officer Dixon, pointing into the house. I noticed he had holstered his weapon, which was a positive sign.

Officer Dixon spoke to him, gesturing with her hands, and then she poked her head inside the doorway.

My heart raced. Had I set everything up perfectly, or had I missed a step?

Officer Dixon stepped back onto the porch and looked at me with a sympathetic expression, offering me a small smile.

I relaxed somewhat. She seemed to take what she had seen inside at face value. For now, at least.

For good measure, I slumped my shoulders and let a few more tears leak out.

She turned away and spoke into her radio. Hopefully, she was calling someone to get Tyler out of my house. I was anxious to clean up the mess he would leave behind.

The crowd had previously consisted of just James and Jake, but over the past few minutes, it had grown into more than a dozen curious onlookers that included both my nosy neighbors and other people who just happened to be driving by and saw the commotion.

Some snapped photos or took videos with their cell phones raised. Some aimed their cameras at me, while others faced the front of the house.

Cars had blocked one side of the street, and officers tried to get traffic moving again. After resorting to threats to arrest people, they finally got it cleared.

I had mixed feelings about this. I didn't want to be a celebrity. I'd done this to save my family, my daughter most of all.

However, having a dozen or more witnesses to my bruised and battered face couldn't hurt. Sympathy from the public would only help my case, I reasoned.

Maybe this was a good thing after all.

The crowd out by the sidewalk suddenly scattered, and a familiar blue pickup truck raced down the street.

Grant had arrived.

I could only assume James had called him after I'd asked him to. James would have had Grant's phone number. We had a phone directory for the neighborhood watch society.

Without even bothering to turn off the ignition, Grant leaped from the truck, ran over to me, and fell to his knees at my feet.

He took in my battered face, my torn shirt, and the blood that was, by now, smeared all over my face, neck, and arms.

"Kat, baby. Sweetheart. What happened? Who did this to you?" he cried, gently taking my hands in his.

After giving them a light squeeze, he let go of one and tentatively reached to stroke the unharmed side of my face.

I leaned my cheek into his hand for comfort.

This wasn't acting; I was so grateful to see him.

Unable to speak, I burst out in tears again, this time genuine.

I raised my arms, and he scooped me carefully out of the seat and into a bear hug, careful not to put any pressure on my injured cheek.

"Kat, my only love. Don't cry. I'm here now, and everything will be fine," he whispered.

I prayed he was right. The rest of our lives together depended on it.

CHAPTER 59

I stood quietly, with Grant's arms around me protectively, on our front lawn as the paramedics rolled Tyler's lifeless body out of the house on a wheeled stretcher.

The sight of Tyler zipped in a black vinyl body bag didn't make me feel guilty. Right then, I didn't feel anything except this pain in my cheek.

I thought I might feel some regret later, but I doubted it.

Tyler had left me no choice.

Any anxiety I felt was no more than my fear of being caught and the stress of trying to remember each detail of my story perfectly.

Grant's hand tightened in mine as the paramedics loaded the body into an ambulance. He had only left my side one to get his phone from the truck. He had made a brief call to Jason and asked him to pick up Kara at school and take her back to his dorm room and to please keep Kara close to him and away from the internet or television until he heard from Grant or me.

I could hear Jason protesting, frantically asking questions, as Grant ended the call.

Without going into great detail, I'd whispered in Grant's ear that Tyler had come into our home and attacked me in our bedroom, intent on having sex with me, and then knocked me into the doorframe when I resisted his advances.

I told Grant I'd managed to push Tyler off me and ran away, but Tyler had chased me and fell down the stairs to his death.

I leaked a few fresh tears as I relayed my story.

Grant's fists clenched, and his face darkened with fury, but he didn't push me for any more information.

I scanned the crowd, seeing some familiar faces but many more that weren't. The number of onlookers had grown even larger over the past hour, and it looked like someone had tipped off the media.

A news van from the local station had set up its cameras on the lawn across the street. A female reporter was clipping on her mike, and another harried-looking man shouted orders to the camera operators. It looked like we were going to be on television.

Thankfully, Officer Gale came out of the front door and motioned for Grant and me to come over. We went up to the porch, where he waited.

"You folks can go inside but stay in the kitchen and living room area. Use the bathroom off the foyer if you need it. Don't go down the hall or up the stairs to the bedroom. We're still processing in those areas, but we figured you'd want to get away from the circus outside."

I spoke. "Please, officer, can I get some clean clothes? These are..." I let my voice trail off as I looked down at my torn and bloody shirt.

Officer Gale considered a minute before replying. "I'll get a female officer to go upstairs in a few minutes and grab you something, okay? I'm sorry, but we really need to keep the scene intact up there until the techs are done."

Grant put his arm around my shoulders as he answered for me. "Yes, sir, that's fine. We'll be in the living room if you need us."

With that, Grant ushered me to the sofa. As I collapsed onto the soft cushions, he grabbed a light throw blanket from the back of the couch and handed it to me. Then he moved back to stand in the doorway, preventing anyone from seeing me undressing.

How ironic.

"Sweetheart, take off your shirt and pants and wrap yourself in that blanket, just until they bring you down some clothes. I'll make sure no one sees you. When you get done, I'll get you a wet towel to wash up. Can I get you anything else, some water, maybe? Coffee?"

I smiled my thanks but shook my head as I began to strip the torn and bloody clothes from my body.

He watched silently as I undressed, lost in his thoughts. Deep furrows lined his brow.

I suppressed the urge to chuckle. Earlier, I'd stripped for one man, and less than two hours later, there I was, undressing for another.

I pushed that strange thought aside and focused on my husband once more. How I adored him. How foolish and shallow I'd been, when I had this magnificent man coming home to me every day.

I would have to do everything in my power to keep this massive secret and make sure I'd get away with what I'd done.

Grant deserved better than me, and when all this was over, I'd spend every day of the rest of our lives showing him how much I loved and needed him.

A few minutes later, Grant returned from the kitchen with a warm, wet washcloth and a glass of ice water. He also carried a half-empty bottle of red wine and two glasses, which he set on the coffee table in front of me.

He offered me a crooked smile and said, "I may need this, even if you don't."

Instead of responding, I gave him another weak smile and patted his knee.

Talking hurt. My whole face was throbbing, and I wished I had thought to ask him for some aspirin.

We spent the next hour mostly in silence, holding hands as we sat on the sofa, waiting.

Assorted types and ranks of police officers went by, some in uniform, some in jackets and slacks.

Occasionally one poked their head into the room and asked if we needed anything.

We didn't. I just wanted them all to leave.

I was surprised Grant didn't ask me more questions, but I was supposed to be traumatized from my ordeal, so he was probably being considerate of my mental state and didn't want to push.

He sat with me, deep in thought, and sipped wine. One glass turned into two, then three. By the time he finished the third glass, I finally felt his muscles relax a little.

After what seemed like hours later, Officer Dixon came into the room.

I had fallen asleep on Grant's shoulder, so I was startled awake when she discreetly cleared her throat from the doorway.

"Kat, Mr. Browne, I think we're just about done here. You'll need to come to the station tomorrow for your official statement, but everything we've seen so far tracks with what you've told us happened here today."

Officer Dixon moved closer to the sofa, and I saw she held two small white cards. She handed one to Grant as he stood.

She explained what they were. "One of these is the contact information for a victim's advocate we work with and recommend to people who have gone through similar traumas. I strongly suggest you make an appointment with her when you're back on your feet. Talking through this with a professional may help. The other card is for a company that comes in and cleans up after these... situations." She stumbled over the last word.

Situation, indeed. The crisis counselor's card would go straight into the garbage. There was no way I'd be telling this story again after tomorrow. Retelling any lie too many times left room for mistakes to be made.

I would save the card for the clean-up company, though. I wanted all traces of Tyler out of my house as soon as possible.

CHAPTER 60

Finally, the police finished with our house. They shuffled around the rooms, gathering and packing up their gear.

When Grant closed the door behind the last officer, he found me standing at the base of the staircase, gazing down at Tyler's blood still pooling on the smooth wooden floorboards. The police had tried not to step in it, but I could see footprints around the stairs.

I felt a sudden rush of nausea and had to reach for the newel post to steady myself.

No matter my reasons or how I justified it, I had taken a life; I'd killed another human being.

Bile rose in my throat as I remembered the crunch of his bones when he landed.

What if I was wrong? What if his threats were empty, a tactic to get me to do what he wanted? Would he have turned his attention to my underaged daughter?

I'd probably never know. I'd done what I needed to with the information I had.

Behind me, I heard the deadbolt on the front door slide home with a thud and then Grant's soft footsteps as he came up next to me.

He pressed his hand gently on the small of my back. "Kat? Let's go up to bed, my love. You look like you're about to faint. I'll set the bedroom to rights while you shower and get cleaned up. Sound good?"

He took my hand in his, and I let him lead me carefully up the stairs, one step at a time, as if I were made of glass.

~

Later, after the paramedics patched up my face, we lay together in the silence of our bedroom, the sound of Grant's even breathing soothing me.

Was it truly over?

I knew I had the police interview the next day, but I felt so relieved that this part was done.

I wasn't sure I could go through with the plan until I saw Tyler climbing the stairs toward me, his dark, dark eyes focused on my naked skin.

I imagined him turning those eyes on Kara; that was all the motivation I needed to give him one hard push.

"Kat?" I heard Grant's whisper reach across to me in the darkness. "Are you awake?"

"Yes," I whispered back.

I'd hoped he'd already fallen asleep. Talking made my face ache, even after six aspirins.

"Do you think you'll have trouble sleeping up here, you know, where it happened?" he asked in a low voice.

"No, I think I'm so exhausted I could sleep anywhere. We'll see how it goes."

He sighed. "No. I don't mean just tonight. I was thinking earlier, if you decide you don't want to sleep up here anymore, we can move into the guest suite downstairs and maybe turn this into a game room or home theater."

He was so, so good to me.

"Maybe so. We can talk about that tomorrow."

Even as I said the words, I knew I wasn't giving up my bedroom. This was my sanctuary, my safe haven.

Despite what Grant thought, no assault had happened there unless you counted me murdering Tyler. Technically, that hadn't happened in the room anyway.

"Kat… I'm so sorry for this. I wish I had been here. I wish I had been able to see what kind of person he was before something like this happened. I could tell you didn't like him. I should have asked why. I should have done… something."

Grant sounded as if he was close to tears, so I scooted over toward him and rested my good cheek on his chest, reaching up to intertwine my fingers in his hair.

"Grant, it's not your fault. It's over now. Tomorrow we'll talk to the police and get it cleared up. Then we'll get back to our life, okay?"

Grant didn't respond right away.

He was so quiet I thought he'd fallen asleep.

"Kat?" he said in another whisper.

"Yes?" I answered patiently, even though I was past ready to get some sleep. I knew some things were easier to talk about in the dark.

"Did Tyler… do anything to you that you haven't told me about? Something that you didn't tell the police?" he asked.

The fear in his voice hurt my heart.

"I wouldn't let him touch me. That's why I ran. He only put his hands on me when he smashed my face."

I could give my husband this half-truth if it helped him get through this.

Another silence.

"Were you scared?" Grant's voice came again in the dark.

"I was terrified. That was the scariest thing I've ever been through."

This, too, was the truth.

Finally, Grant whispered softly, "Okay. I love you, Kat."

"I love you, too. Always have, always will."

Soon after, I heard his breathing even out in sleep.

CHAPTER 61

Grant and I arrived at the police station promptly at ten the following day, as they'd asked us to do. Neither of us had spoken much on the drive over. Each lost in our thoughts. I went over my story in my head, checking for plot holes or mistakes in my timeline.

I'd gone back and read over Tyler's texts, and his messages all supported my version of what had happened yesterday, as did my replies.

Tyler had been stalking me; this much was true.

How it started and ended was what I had to be careful about in the retelling. One slip-up could bring this whole house of cards crashing down around me.

As soon as we walked into the station's reception area, the desk clerk recognized us, and we were hurriedly ushered into an interview room. I wasn't surprised. The news coverage from the day before was on all the local news channels and websites.

I looked around, taking in the ugly green cinder block walls, cheap laminate furniture, and bad lighting. The room looked just as stark and terrifying as every interrogation room I'd ever seen on television.

I noted one professional-looking video camera set up on the table in front of me and another mounted on the wall above our heads. I arranged myself in the chair, so my battered side faced the camera lens.

I caught myself picking at the loose edge of the table and had to force myself to stop. Fidgeting people were usually nervous people.

I'd have to remember not to bite my fingernails or tap my fingers on the table.

Even though I wasn't a suspect, at least not yet, I knew they'd be watching me for any tell-tale clues.

Soon the door opened, and someone entered.

A new detective had been assigned to my case. He was tall, with startling blue eyes contrasting his silver hair. There was an air of authority about him that made me nervous. I had the feeling this man had seen it all.

Suddenly, I was terrified that he'd be able to look right into my soul and know the terrible thing I'd done, the lies I'd told. I tried to shake off the fear and concentrate on what was coming.

I had decided it would be a good idea to dress conservatively for this interview. I needed to look more like an average middle-aged housewife and less like a woman who got naked for strangers.

From my closet, I'd carefully chosen unflattering black slacks and a shapeless cream-colored top. Neither did anything for my figure or complexion. I was going for matron, not seductress.

The silver-haired man sat across from us and introduced himself.

"Mrs. Browne, Mr. Browne, I'm Detective Charles. It's good to meet you both, although I wish it was under better circumstances. Now, we're going to ask you to tell us what happened, starting with you finding the suspect in your bedroom. Go slow, and let me know if you need to take a break at any time, okay?"

I nodded, and he went on.

"Mr. Browne, please don't interrupt or add anything while your wife is speaking. We'll have some questions for you after we're done with Mrs. Browne."

With a curt nod, Grant indicated that he understood, and we began.

I weaved my tale with watery eyes, clutching a tissue to my nose as I relayed the story from the beginning.

I'd gone over the events so many times that the lies had nearly become the truth in my mind. I addressed the camera and told my version of events.

Tyler had met our son Jason in the club where Jason worked after helping Jason get home following getting sick. They'd struck up a friendship, and Jason had brought Tyler home a few times for dinner because Tyler didn't know anyone in the area, and Jason felt sorry for him.

During these visits, Tyler had apparently developed some sort of crush on me and sent flowers and gifts to the house and a series of suggestive text messages.

I tried to firmly reject him, but he was persistent. I added that Tyler had found excuses to come by when no one was home but I didn't let him in.

The silver-haired detective taking my statement interrupted me when I got to this part of the story. "Mrs. Browne, why didn't you tell your son what was going on? Or your husband?"

I had already prepared an answer to this very question.

"I really thought Tyler just had a crush on me. He was so young. I didn't want to embarrass him, and I knew if I told Grant of my concerns, Grant would have confronted Tyler. I figured his attachment to me would run its course, nothing would need to be done, and no one would be embarrassed in the end. Now, I wish I had said something, but I never imagined Tyler would be violent. Maybe if I'd spoken up at the beginning, he would still be alive."

I dropped my head and let the tears flow.

Then I walked him through how the assault happened, step by step, relaying how I had been home alone, with Grant at work and Kara at school.

While I was upstairs making my bed, I heard footsteps behind me, and I turned to find Tyler in my room, and that was when he assaulted me, pushing me down on the bed and tried to tear my clothes off.

I told the officer that when I ran, Tyler had grabbed me by the hair and slammed my face into the doorframe.

When I was done, he asked me a few questions about our regular life, taking notes as I answered.

He asked about our kids, their schools, Grant's work, and what kind of security system we had at the house.

I explained that we had an older one, but it hadn't worked in years, and we'd never gotten around to replacing it. I almost felt the detective's disappointment in the lack of video footage.

In the end, my injuries were consistent with my story, and the position of Tyler's body when they found him did make it appear as though he'd fallen, giving chase to me after the assault upstairs in the bedroom.

My explanation must have seemed plausible, as Grant was allowed to take me home shortly after.

No charges were filed against me.

The whole thing was determined to be a tragic accident. I was free.

CHAPTER 62

Despite not having much regret over killing Tyler, I did have other regrets.

I had caused damage to my family, even if I had made a choice for the right reasons.

We had yet to sit down with Kara and Jason and tell them what had happened to Tyler, and I was not looking forward to lying to my children, even for their own good.

Grant and I had gotten at least a dozen text messages from each while we were at the police station, so as soon as we arrived at the house, I called Jason and told him it was okay for him and Kara to return home.

All I told him was that something had happened yesterday, but his father and I were both fine.

As we waited for them to show up, I went into the hall bathroom the kids used. I leaned over the sink to peer at my bruised cheek in the mirror.

That side of my face had turned several unattractive shades of blue and purple. I gingerly touched the area and winced at the sharp pain, idly wondering if I'd have a permanent scar there.

I shrugged. A scar would be a small price to pay for getting away with murder.

Still, I made a mental note to consult with a plastic surgeon.

An hour later, Jason burst through the front door with Kara on his heels. Wide-eyed, he flew into the kitchen, where Grant and I sat waiting at the table.

We each had a glass of wine in front of us, and an empty glass was waiting for Jason at his usual place. I had a feeling my son would soon need a drink.

Seeing my bruised face, Jason exclaimed, "Mom! What happened to your cheek? Are you okay?"

He looked around wildly, and his gaze landed on his father. Eyes narrowed, he asked, "Dad... did... did you...?"

Kara stood behind him, still and silent, only her eyes in motion, moving from me to her father and back.

I realized what Jason assumed, so I quickly rushed to reassure him before Grant could react. The last thing we needed then was a quarrel amongst the family.

"Jason! No! Your father has never raised a hand to me and never would. Sit down, both of you, and let us explain."

I gestured to the empty chairs across from Grant and me.

"I'm going to tell you what happened here yesterday, and I'd appreciate it if you'd let me finish before you start asking a bunch of questions, okay?"

My words were firm, but my tone was gentle.

Jason nodded and slumped into a chair, his eyes never leaving my face.

Kara looked as though she wanted to bolt down the hall to her room, but before I could ask her again to sit, Grant spoke to them.

"Jason, you know I'd never hurt your mother. Kara, please sit down and listen to your mom. She has been through something terrible, and she needs you and your brother to be here for her right now."

Kara sat. She nervously chewed on her thumbnail, a lifetime habit of hers that she'd always done when she was upset.

Now came the hard part. Taking a deep breath, I began. "Jason, I know how hard this is going to be for you to hear, and I want to tell you first that I am so sorry. If I could have done anything to change what happened, I would have."

This was true. Hindsight, again.

"Yesterday, while your father was at work and I was here alone, Tyler came into our house and attacked me in our bedroom."

Jason stayed silent, but Kara let out a gasp. "What do you mean, attacked?"

Grant spoke up, "Let your mother finish, Kara."

She shot him a dirty look but said nothing further, so I went on.

"It seems as if Tyler had developed some sort of a crush on me. He sent me some gifts and things and a few texts that were inappropriate, but I didn't tell anyone because I thought he would just get over it, and no one would ever need to know. When he came into the house yesterday, he tried to force me to have sex with him. I refused him, and we fought. He took me by the hair and slammed me into the door, and I ran downstairs to get away from him."

Again, I reached up and gently touched two fingers to my cheek.

I choked up, knowing I had yet to tell Jason the worst part. I steeled myself for his reaction and continued. "Tyler tried to chase me down the stairs, but he stumbled and fell down to the bottom. Jason... I'm sorry, Tyler is dead."

For a moment, all was quiet. The air was charged with tension, but no one spoke.

Then Jason shocked me by slamming his hands down on the table.

He shot to his feet and yelled, "I knew it! I knew something was up with him. He talked about you all the time, always asking questions about you and making weird comments until I finally told him to shut up about you already. I should have known it was more than making small talk. I can't believe I brought that crazy bastard into our house. I'm so sorry I didn't protect you, Mom."

I was stunned. My son was never angry and hardly ever raised his voice unless he was excited about something.

Now I did feel guilt.

Jason hadn't brought Tyler into our home. I had done that.

He came to my side of the table and crouched next to me. He put one hand on top of mine resting on the table and said softly, "Mom, I'm so sorry for all of this. I would kill him if he wasn't already dead for what he did to you."

This time the tears that flooded my eyes were genuine.

My beautiful boy.

If I never did another good thing in my life, I knew I'd done right with Jason. His compassion and love for me shone in his eyes, and at that moment, I was glad for what I'd done to save this family.

I put my hand on the back of his head and touched our foreheads together. "Thank you," I whispered.

Tyler wasn't good enough to be friends with my son. He had drugged Jason, led my daughter on, and threatened to do worse.

I'd done this for them.

There was a tiny part of me that, only in the deepest, darkest hours of the night, could admit I might have done it a little for myself, too.

Tyler's death benefited us all.

From across the table, Kara said, "May I be excused? I'd like to be alone for a little while if that's okay," in a tiny voice.

It was plain to see how hurt Kara was by this news. She looked like she'd been dealt one fine blow between the eyes.

Grant assured her that it was all right with us if she left, and he lifted his arms as though to offer her a comforting hug, but Kara shrugged away from him and moved toward the hall.

At the doorway, she surprised me by pausing and looking back at me, and I saw her eyes glistening with unshed tears.

"I'm glad you're okay, Momma." She hadn't called me that in years.

And then she was gone.

CHAPTER 63

What happened with Tyler changed us all.

In a way, all four of us were more careful with each other and considerate of the other person's feelings and needs.

Kara spoke more respectfully to Grant and me but kept to herself a bit more than before.

Ironically, I'd catch her journaling late into the night, even though she previously had no interest in doing so.

Jason made an effort to come home more often, and if he couldn't call, he'd text at least once or twice a day. He quit his job at the club and got a part-time position with a commercial janitorial crew, working evenings and weekends.

As for Grant and me, well, things were odd between us.

He was still handling me with extreme care, which I'd expected after what I'd been through. But sometimes, when he thought I wasn't paying attention to him, I'd catch him looking at me as though I was a puzzle he needed to solve.

We hadn't had sex since Tyler died, but Grant was still affectionate in other ways. He'd hug or kiss me multiple times a day, just as he had before. But it was clear something between us had changed.

I was beginning to wonder if the idea of Tyler laying his hands on me had made me less attractive to Grant in some way. I hoped it was no more than that and he wasn't suspicious about the story I told that day.

I didn't bring it up. I thought things would even out as time passed. *Let sleeping dogs lie.*

Grant and I decided that once I was fully healed, we'd plan a family beach vacation. We'd pack up the kids and go somewhere sunny and warm. We'd lie on the beach and play in the surf, leaving behind the memories of Tyler and what had happened to him in our home.

And so, life went on, only slightly different than before.

I'd killed a man to save my family and had gotten away with it so far.

PART THREE

CHAPTER 64

Tyler

I'm not a bad guy. I am a voyeur.

In simple terms, what that means is that I enjoy looking at women in various stages of undress and watching them disrobe. I don't need to have sex with them. The watching is what gets me off.

Back in the day, they called people like me Peeping Toms. That's not really a correct description, though. I'm not skulking around in the dark. I also don't mind when the women watch me watching them.

The first time I spied the red-haired woman undressing in her window, I was instantly aroused.

When I see a woman undress accidentally, it's a thousand times more satisfying than when it's staged.

From that distance, I couldn't tell her age. I just saw her pale, creamy skin forming a stunning backdrop for her fiery hair.

She could have been twenty or fifty. It didn't matter that she was sweaty and wearing exercise clothes. In my eyes, she was exquisite.

Redheads have always been my favorite, especially if they're natural.

Bonus points if they match: above and below.

When the woman in the window saw me watching, I sent her a quick reassuring smile. I hated the idea that she might be embarrassed for exposing herself to me in her natural state.

I yearn for the world to normalize undressing for strangers, for pleasure. I don't consider this taboo, even though that seems to be the popular opinion. After all, we were born naked.

In my eyes, what I do is way hotter and much safer than having actual sex because I can maintain the mystery aspect. I can take part this way with little to no feelings involved, there's zero chance of getting a disease, and there are none of the commitment issues that are so common with mainstream dating.

But the world isn't ready for voyeurs. I'd been scorned more than once when I tried to explain what I liked and wanted to a woman I'd been dating. Tired of being rejected and labeled a pervert, it soon became easier to pay for what I needed instead of being ridiculed for my preferences.

People always tend to be afraid of what doesn't fit into their perception of "normal," they hate anything that they can't stuff into their neat little boxes of what they call acceptable behavior.

Anyway, after she saw me watching that first day, she hurried to close her window shades, and I assumed that was the end of it.

I was disappointed and wished I'd been close enough to see her cheeks and chest flush with the delicious pink color of embarrassment.

But it was what it was.

I'd be around for a while, doing odd handyman work for the old guy who owned the house behind hers, but I figured she'd avoid me at all costs.

The next day, I glanced up at her window and saw her watching me work again.

Now, I know I'm good-looking. I'm fully aware of my effect on women, and I use my looks as a weapon when needed.

She was likely a bored housewife with a neglectful husband, so if watching me sweat in the sun gave her a little break from her otherwise dull life, who was I to deny her?

But she kept showing up each morning, just standing there watching me toil in the hot sun. I'd smile or wave to her to be friendly and let her know I saw her and didn't mind the audience.

Once or twice, I thought it would be nice if she'd brought me a cold drink, and I could get a look at her up close. She never did, though, not even after we started our game. I guess she didn't want to ruin the illusion.

After about two weeks of this, I decided to try to play with the woman a bit. This guy's yard was a mess, and I was growing tired of busting my ass out here every day, with no change in routine, and for very little money. The old guy was a cheapskate, but I needed the cash.

Paying for my habit isn't cheap.

One morning, I waited until I saw her gaze directed at me to have a little fun with the redhead and amuse myself.

When our eyes locked, I pointed at my chest and hers. After a moment, she held her hands up as if to say she didn't understand, so I did it again—this time she understood.

To my shock and extreme pleasure, after a long pause, she peeled off her tank top, exposing her sports bra above her toned stomach.

Splendid is what she was. After spending so many days watching how she moved and how she reacted, I figured she was somewhere close to forty, maybe.

She was in superior shape for a middle-aged woman, and now the gym clothes made sense. She must be working out somewhere before coming upstairs to shower and change.

I wondered if she went to the gym or if she had a home setup. I imagined sitting in a corner of her gym, watching her exercise, the sweat on her skin beading and then rolling down her body.

Unable to stop myself, I licked my lips. She caught the gesture and looked away. Again, I wished I could see her blush up close.

I thought that would be the end, but for the next few days, she'd appear every weekday morning at around the same time.

I assumed from this that she was married or had kids or both. I never saw her in the window on a Saturday.

One morning, I looked up, and there she stood, tall and proud in a tiny lingerie set.

I blinked hard, scared that I'd had a heat stroke and was hallucinating. But no, I seemed fine, and she was still there, a vision in scraps of lace.

Oh, she wanted to up the ante, did she?

This was getting really, really good. Two could play this game.

As a bonus, I was getting it for free.

CHAPTER 65

Grant

I am not a stupid man.

I first began feeling something was going on with Kat weeks ago.

My wife and I have a normal, healthy physical relationship. She has never been adventurous by any means, but I have no complaints.

Not everyone likes to experiment, and that's always been fine by me, and I've never had the need to look elsewhere for sex.

Kat never claims to "have a headache," and almost any time I'm in the mood, she's always been up for it.

Still, things in the bedroom have become routine to a certain degree. However, I think this is normal when two people have been together since childhood, as she and I have.

But a while ago, out of nowhere, it seemed she was in the mood nearly every night. She'd started waking me up in the middle of the night by climbing on top of me, ready to go. She even occasionally groped me in the kitchen or when passing me in the hallway when the kids weren't looking.

This new version of my wife is a little disturbing and a lot sexy.

My first thought was that she must be having an affair, so I paid closer attention to her.

Over the next few weeks, she started dressing for bed in skimpy, sexy lingerie I'd never seen her wear before. Tiny matching bra and panty sets, with thongs so small I could barely see them.

Don't get me wrong, I loved these changes and took full advantage of them.

I still had concerns that she was seeing someone else.

But then, realistically, when would she have the time? I knew her daily routine and was notified anytime she left the house, thanks to the tracking app we used to monitor the kids' phones and whereabouts. I'd receive an alert on my phone if her car left the house.

The possibility of an affair seemed so impossible, so... unthinkable.

I know Kat. She just isn't the type.

I also know men always say that about their wives, but Kat is different.

She is one of the most giving, selfless people I know, always putting other people's needs ahead of hers.

And then I found Kat's diary, and the truth became clear. Kat always loved putting her thoughts on paper. She had even toyed with the idea of pursuing a journalism career before settling on medicine.

Bedtime would find her scribbling words in her little leather book before she'd lay down her pen and turn off her lamp.

I'd never been tempted to read her journal until now. Her private thoughts were just that, private.

Plus, I thought I already knew everything there was to know about my wife.

When I noticed that her diary was missing from the bedside table where she usually left it, it made me suspicious, so I decided to look for it and see exactly what she was up to.

I waited impatiently for a Saturday when she was out on some errand with Kara. I searched the bedroom and eventually found her diary in her walk-in closet, tucked inside the pocket of a fancy leather coat I'd bought her but had never seen her wear.

Steeling myself for the worst, I sat down to read.

My first reaction was rage. At her. At him.

My wife, my best friend, the mother of my children, and my partner of over twenty years had been purposely showing her body off to another man.

It didn't matter that it was an accident the first time, she could have told me, and we'd have probably laughed about it over dinner.

My second reaction was sadness, mixed with a bit of guilt and some relief.

Had I neglected her, pushed her to this? Was Kat so desperate for attention that she had to perform her own peep show for a stranger?

I re-read a few older entries.

Kat had written that she felt lost, without purpose. She wrote that her life was filled with doing everything for the kids and me, and she had little to nothing that was just for herself.

This broke my heart a little.

I didn't realize how much of Kat's life revolved around us and how little time and effort she set aside for herself. I knew she had regrets about not attending med school, but she didn't bring that up very often, so I didn't either.

I have become complacent and comfortable. Maybe I am guilty of something, too.

I was also relieved that Kat wasn't sleeping with another man. Somehow this made me feel better about what I'd found in her diary.

I'm ashamed to admit it, but my third reaction was arousal.

Even though I was disappointed she'd kept this from me, I was strangely intrigued by what she was doing with him.

There was something empowering about knowing another man was looking at my wife's body and finding pleasure in it but was unable to touch her.

My wife is stunning, all red hair and luscious curves. She was heart-breakingly gorgeous at sixteen, and she still is at forty.

As I realized what she and Tyler were doing had never gone past the point of looking, I found, to my shame, that the idea rather turned me on.

I wondered if I could watch him while he watched her.

I thought it would be like having a wife who was a stripper or dancer and being able to sit in the audience. Knowing no one would touch her except me.

The difference is that Kat did it for confidence and a feeling of self-worth instead of money.

I sat there on the bed for a while, Kat's diary in hand, and I decided not to confront her yet. I would put her diary back where I'd found it and check for new entries whenever I had the opportunity. I could always step in if things went too far.

Besides, an insane idea had planted itself in my mind, and I needed time to think about it.

This plan worked for a while.

Kat carried on with Tyler in what I came to call her "window sessions," and I continued to reap its benefits.

Her underwear got smaller as her confidence and sex drive grew bigger.

Then came the night Tyler first came to our house. Kat hadn't known his name before that night, and neither had I. But I caught his sly looks at her and was aware of her obvious physical signs of distress during dinner that night and afterward.

As I said, I'm not stupid. I put two and two together, and the answer was Tyler was the man outside.

As soon as I could, I checked her diary again, but there was only one entry explaining what had changed between them.

Tyler had pushed Kat too far, and she'd refused him.

I was proud of her for drawing the line, but suddenly the game had become dangerous.

This asshole was now coming to my house, hanging out with our son, and casting his eye on our thirteen-year-old daughter.

I'd seen Kara looking at Tyler in ways that made the hair on my neck stand up, but I didn't see anything improper happen between them.

Then again, I worked long hours and missed much time with my family.

Maybe I'd mention it to Kat and see if she had any thoughts on Kara's obvious "crush" on Tyler.

As intrigued as I was by what Tyler and Kat had been doing, I would not have my daughter involved with this man. Any kind of friendship between the two of them was inappropriate. Besides being way too old for her, Tyler was obviously some sort of freak.

While I tried to figure out a plan, I kept my eye on Kara for any changed behaviors. She seemed to be on her phone slightly more than usual, but checking the app, I saw no new numbers in her contact list.

She seemed unchanged, still annoying her mother and pushing boundaries like every teenage girl. It didn't matter; I wanted Tyler out of our lives.

Now, I'm not a fighter. I'm a thinker and a planner. I don't enjoy confrontation and avoid it whenever possible. I am always most likely to let people do as they please rather than try to sway them to my way of thinking.

When forced to do so, I preferred to use my words, not my fists.

Money was the clear answer here. I had no doubt. I could tell, just by being around Tyler a handful of times, that he was the kind of person who could be bought. I just needed to know his price.

Whatever it was, I'd pay him off, make it worth his while to go away.

I scrolled through Kat's text list on the family app. I jotted down any numbers I wasn't familiar with, and after a few quick searches on my computer later, I tapped out a text to Tyler.

Tyler, this is Grant. Jason's dad. We need to talk. I know what you've been doing with my wife. Meet me at Ramelli's Pizza on Parkside Ave. tomorrow at two o'clock. Trust me, it will be beneficial for both of us for you to show up. Don't respond to this text.

As I'd instructed, no reply came. I was fairly confident he'd show up, for curiosity's sake, if nothing else.

Some say the internet is forever, but that's not quite true. If you, like myself, have a background in internet technology, you know there are ways to make things, emails and the like, disappear from the World Wide Web permanently.

For example, my text message to Tyler.

Opening a secure browser window, I logged into a website I used occasionally and deleted the texts from both my account and Tyler's.

All traces of our communication were gone, and it would take a team of experts to find it, but first, they'd have to know it existed.

Later that afternoon at the office, I told Annie, my administrative assistant, to reschedule my appointments for the next afternoon and block out three hours after lunch, instructing her to log it as a "client presentation."

Annie had been with me for over ten years and had learned to ask no questions. She did as I asked and emailed me the schedule changes.

On my way home that afternoon, I made a detour to the bank.

The teller greeted me with a friendly smile, and I told her I needed to access my safety deposit box. She took my information, and after I waited for a few minutes in the lobby, she returned and asked me to follow her down a short hallway to the vault.

The walls of the vault were lined with numbered boxes of various sizes. She went to a medium-sized one, inserted her key, and motioned for me to put my matching key in the slot. Then she slid the box from the wall and set it on the table behind us.

"Here you go, Mr. Browne. Take all the time you need. When you're done, press the green button on the wall there by the door, and I'll come back to replace your box. Do you have any questions before I go?"

I shook my head and thanked her. "I'm good. I appreciate your help."

Once alone, I lifted the metal lid from the box and peered inside at its contents.

No one knew about this box but the bank and me, even though I had Kat as an emergency contact on the account.

I'm a careful man, a planner, as I said.

Being in the internet technology field for over twenty years, I was more aware than most people of how dangerous the internet and computers could be.

A few keystrokes made by the wrong person and your financial future could be ruined or worse. This box was my safety net for any such occurrence.

There were stacks and stacks of cash, all in hundreds and fifties. I removed one stack and set it to the side.

Beneath the cash were envelopes of documents, including a life insurance policy I had on Kat that she was unaware of.

You can't be too prepared these days.

The last item was a small leather pouch full of flash drives. These were different sorts of insurance policies.

As a little side hobby, for certain special clients, I would make emails, texts, photos, and other such things disappear.

For a price, of course, hence the stacks of untraceable, untaxable cash.

And only after I made copies for myself. I never knew what I'd need in the future, so I kept everything.

I left everything in the box as it was, except the thick pile of bills I had set aside.

Locking the box with my key, I pressed the button to summon the teller.

When she returned, I requested a plain envelope. She was happy to oblige and led me back to the lobby.

A few minutes later, I tucked the fat envelope of cash into my jacket pocket and strolled out of the bank and into the bright afternoon sunlight.

I ran through the list I'd prepared earlier.

Everything was in place.

I also had an idea of how Tyler could earn a fat bonus, in addition to his payoff to disappear.

The seed that had been planted when I read her diary had become full-grown. I wondered what he'd think of my proposal. I found myself eager for this meeting.

CHAPTER 66

Tyler

I read the text message from Grant twice. *Huh. Interesting.*

I pace in a tight square, trying to figure out his motive for wanting to meet.

My apartment is not much larger than a walk-in closet, so each trip only takes seconds.

I can stretch my arms and almost touch the walls on either side. My second or third-hand sofa doubles as my bed, and my tiny refrigerator sits on a rickety table next to an electric one-burner hot plate. Sometimes the appliances work, but mostly they don't.

The view from my window isn't nearly as enticing as the view into Kat's, just the plain brick wall of the apartment building next to mine. I don't even have the benefit of any windows to look through across the way.

Anyway, I'd pretty much exhausted all the cash jobs I could find in this backwoods town. I'll probably need to consider moving on soon. There isn't much to pack, as I tend to travel light. I never know when I'd have to leave a place in a hurry.

Back to Grant.

The man didn't sound angry, and I was intrigued by what he would want to talk with me about since somehow, he'd found out about Kat and me.

He certainly isn't dumb enough to try to fight me in a pizza joint in full view of other people.

I chuckle dryly at the image of him and me wrestling among discarded pizza crusts and spilled drinks.

Most likely, he just wants to warn me away from his wife. That is fine. I am growing tired of chasing her anyway.

I thought I could bully her into finishing our game by using a few scare tactics, but so far, she has resisted.

As much as I want to see Kat completely nude, there are numerous other ways to get women to take off their clothes for me the way I like.

I could hunt through my favorite websites for a woman who resembles her, arrange a meeting, and that should scratch the itch.

But the thing is, I am intrigued by Kat, and not just by her body.

I want to hear her voice and smell her scent. I want to know what she does with her time when she isn't in the window.

To satisfy my curiosity, one morning, instead of showing up to work in the yard, I parked down the street and watched her front door until she came outside.

As she got in her car and drove off, I followed her.

We drove downtown to some preppy café. I parked in a nearby lot, and from across the street, I watched her through the plate glass window as she enjoyed a leisurely lunch with a friend.

I was mesmerized by her delicate fingers as she used her fork and knife to cut her food. She had no idea how stunning she was as she laughed with her friend, tossing back her long red hair.

I had to force myself to walk away from the view; it wouldn't do to develop an attachment to Kat. I reminded myself that my need for her was basic and primal, not emotional.

Anyway, I have to admit, I did do a little light flirting with Kara.

I didn't take it too far, though, and I only sent her a handful of text messages, despite her many, many texts to me after we met at dinner.

Regardless of what I said to Kat, I would never touch her daughter. Kids weren't my thing, and I hold nothing but disgust for pedophiles. Now, that is sick and unnatural.

I also arranged to "accidentally" meet Jason in the bar where he worked. Finding him wasn't that difficult. I had been watching Kat's house since she denied me what was mine. I saw the tall, cheerful-looking guy go into the house with a basket full of clothes and figured it had to be her kid.

A few nights later, I followed him to the club.

I thought he was just there getting a drink, but the fact that he worked there made my plan even better.

Okay, so I may have spiked his drink to make myself useful to him and begin a friendship. The dose I slipped into his beer wasn't going to truly hurt him. It was just enough so that I could play the hero.

I also may have used the I-don't-know anyone-in-town card, so he'd feel sorry for me and invite me to dinner at his parents' house a few times.

Don't get me wrong, Jason is a cool guy. We spent many nights hanging out, drinking beers, and talking about women.

Of course, I didn't let on that it was his mother who I wanted to see naked. Jason wasn't that easy-going, I'm pretty sure no one would be.

At any rate, in another life, Jason and I could have formed a strong friendship, but that's not my goal here. I just want what his mother promised me, and I'll be on my merry way out of all their lives for good.

I check my phone for the time. It is time to get ready for my meeting with Grant.

CHAPTER 67

Grant

I tap my foot impatiently beneath the tablecloth as I wait for Tyler to arrive.

To pass the time, I survey my surroundings. It isn't an upscale eatery by any means, but Ramelli's is still much nicer than most neighborhood pizza joints.

A waitress comes by and asks if I'd like to look at a menu. I decline food but ask for a cup of black coffee.

With a nod, she smiles at me and returns to the counter.

I look around once more.

I'll have to bring Kat here once this is all over. Maybe do a date night out.

I think she'd enjoy the vintage feel of the place. The leather of the booths is in good condition, free of cracks, and there is decent art on the walls. The red and white checkered tablecloths so common in pizza parlors top the wooden tables.

Most of the booths and tables were full, with people of all ages enjoying their pies. I can hear orders being called out in the open kitchen.

The place has a homey and inviting feel to it.

My musing is interrupted by the jangling of the small metal bell someone had tied to the entrance door.

I glance up, and Tyler is scanning the room for me.

I'd picked a busy time of day, wanting him to be comfortable knowing he is safe in a crowd of people.

As Tyler spots me, I lift a hand in a brief greeting and wait for him to make his way to where I sit.

He weaves through the tables toward me, and I see a group of teenage girls eye him and try to hide their giggles behind their hands.

He notices the girls, too, sending a smile and a smolder in their general direction.

Resisting the urge to roll my eyes, I wait as he reaches my table and drops into a chair across from me.

Neither of us say anything for a minute, and the tension is palpable.

Tyler and I have never been alone before, and I imagine he must be nervous since I have divulged that I knew what he and Kat had been up to.

I am determined to maintain the upper hand in this conversation, so I let the silence drag on until it gets awkward enough that Tyler is finally forced to speak first.

"So, I'm here. What is it you wanted to see me about?"

Just then, the waitress returns with my cup of coffee. She sets it down and, with her friendly smile in place, turns to see who has joined me.

Taking in his handsome face, she stammers. "Um... hi. Can I get you anything? Anything at all?"

Tyler requests ice water with lemon and thanks her, adding a saucy wink.

The waitress blushes and scampers off to do his bidding. *Jesus.*

Despite what I am about to ask Tyler to do, I want to smash his smug face in.

I have to remind myself what my goals are for this meeting.

"Here's the thing, Tyler. It doesn't matter how, but I found out about what you and Kat were doing in the window. I know it ended because you pushed her beyond what she was comfortable with, but I don't care about that. Consider yourself lucky you didn't touch her, and that's all I have to say about that. What I do care about is you leaving my family alone for good, which includes Jason and Kara, too. I've seen the way my daughter looks at you, and I'm telling you now, I will not stand for it."

I pause here and take a sip of my now lukewarm coffee, waiting for his response.

Tyler's eyes narrow, and I can see him weighing my words.

He leans back in his chair, kicking one leg out insolently, as he grins slyly at me, and asks, "And why would I do that?"

Again, I want to beat him to a bloody pulp.

"Because I'm going to make it worth your while. I'm prepared to pay you to disappear from all of our lives."

His gaze grows hungry.

Ah, there it is. I knew this is the right thing to do. Money is such an efficient motivator for scum like Tyler.

"Well, Grant, exactly how much are you prepared to pay?" he demands, sarcastically mocking my words.

I let that pass without comment and open my suit jacket slightly, allowing him a glimpse of the fat bank envelope tucked in the inside pocket.

"Five thousand dollars," I reply, closing my jacket and refastening the button. "Cash."

He straightens in his seat and sticks his hand out for me to shake. "Deal."

I knew I had him. Seeing that I'd brought the cash, Tyler must know I am serious about this.

All that money is within his reach. All he has to do is agree to my terms.

I am rather surprised he doesn't try to squeeze more from me by offering a counter-deal, though. He must be pretty desperate for money.

"Slow down a minute. I'm not done."

I raise a hand to tell him to wait, but he leans forward and asks, "What else, man? I just said I'd do it. I'm gone. Give me the cash."

Again, he puts a hand out.

I let out a laugh.

This is too easy. If he wants the money that badly, he'll likely jump at my next proposal.

"Just listen. To be honest with you, I knew about you and Kat way before she ended it. At first, I was angry and considered hurting you, but truthfully, I find it somewhat... intriguing. Don't ask questions. My reasons are my own."

I can see the surprise in his eyes, but he doesn't interrupt.

I continue. "So, I want you to do it one more time. I want you to get Kat to undress for you. Completely. And I want to watch."

Tyler is already shaking his head. "No way, dude, I'm not into that kind of thing. Threesomes are out of the question. I do my thing one-on-one."

I wait for him to stop talking and then go on. "Hear me out. I won't be there with the two of you. I want you to convince Kat to play the game one more time. I'll have a camera set up in our bedroom that will video it, and I'll watch it later, in my own time."

I pull a folded wad of cash from the pocket of my slacks. "This is ten thousand dollars. You'd get the whole fifteen grand after I verify the video was taken."

Tyler licks his lips as he stares at the cash.

He raises his eyes to meet mine and then frowns as he says, "It won't work. I've been trying to get her to keep playing our game, but she's done with me. There's no way she'd agree to strip nude. That's exactly what I tried to get her to do before, and she decided to end it with me instead. What makes you think she'd agree now?"

I smile. "I've already thought of that. You'll tell Kat that if she doesn't do it, then you'll expose her to me, no pun intended. Threaten that you'll tell me everything, every single dirty detail of what she's done in the window for you. Since she has no idea that I already know, I do believe she'll go for it. She'll agree, you'll arrange the meeting, and I'll set up the camera. I want it done in the bedroom. There's a bookcase full of clutter where I can easily hide the camera. It's very small."

He looks at me almost with admiration. "Damn, dude. That is some dirty shit you're doing to your wife. You realize you're basically paying me to blackmail her. Also, what if the threat of you finding out isn't enough?"

"I'm sure you can convince her. I'd never have thought she'd start this up with you in the first place, but apparently, you had some kind of sick hold on her. Tell her whatever you need to so she'll say yes. Make sure she knows this is the end, that she'll never see you again after it happens. I believe that's all she really wants anyway."

I lean back and steeple my fingers over my chest. "One more thing. You don't touch her. If you lay one finger on her, I'll beat you to death, and you won't get a dime. Do we have an agreement?"

Tyler grins and extends his hand to me one final time.

"Absolutely."

CHAPTER 68

Tyler

I still can't believe Kat agreed.

It seems too good to be true that I'll get what I want from her and walk away with fifteen thousand dollars from her husband.

I'm suspicious by nature, so I've looked at this from all possible angles, but I can't find a downside.

Now, I'm not a man of great conscience, but I did feel like an asshole for the comments I made to Kat about Kara. I justified it by reminding myself that Grant had told me to do whatever it took to convince her, so technically, I was following his instructions.

He probably won't like it if he knew I had used Kara to get Kat to agree to my demands, though.

Honestly, I really do want to get Kat naked. I assumed when we started our game that we would work up to a complete reveal. That's how it is done.

When she started undressing more and more each day, I figured she knew the rules.

I've spent many long nights in my crappy closet of an apartment, dreaming of playing out the finale with Kat.

And then, of course, there is the money.

I can almost feel how the stacks of cash Grant has shown me will fit in my pockets.

The timing of Grant's proposal is near perfect. I have all but exhausted my financial prospects around here. Fifteen thousand should get me started up nicely wherever I land next.

Grant's second request had been a surprise. Not the payoff part; rich guys always throw money at problems they want solved.

His proposal, though, blew my mind.

Grant had seemed so… straight. So conservative. Like he'd never done a bad thing in his life.

I guess you never really know people.

But like I said, I'm not one to kink-shame. If the guy wants to watch his wife strip for me, I'll be more than happy to accommodate.

Especially since I'll be so handsomely compensated.

Grant and I decided to meet up at the same pizza joint a few days later.

By that time, he'd have watched the video, and hopefully satisfied, Grant would hand over my money, and I'd be gone.

Although… I wonder if somehow, I can get my hands on a copy of the video. That could come in handy if, at a later date, I find myself in financial straits again.

I bet Grant would be willing to pay big to keep Kat from finding out that he'd set her up so he could watch us. How much would my silence be worth?

I'll have to think about that more later.

~

I arrive in Kat's neighborhood a few minutes early.

As she has instructed, I park a few blocks down and set out on foot for her house. Seeing no one around, I go around the side of the house to the back gate like I'd done before and as she'd told me to do.

I stand near the pool in the backyard, where she'll be able to see me when she comes to the window.

At eleven on the dot, Kat appears. *This is happening.*

I realize I'd been waiting for either Kat to back out on our deal or to find out it is all some kind of setup, like maybe Grant will let me walk into the house, and then he'll be waiting to kick my ass.

But no. There she is, centered in her window, rays of light playing on her skin as she stands, chin up, eyes cast down in my direction.

She is a vision. Her flame-colored curls flow over her shoulders, brushing the tops of her breasts.

This is the stuff dreams and adult movies are made of.

Kat is magnificent.

I remind myself this is my only chance at this and to not rush through the experience. I want to savor every moment, and I want to give Grant his money's worth. I still have the possibility of future financial extortion in the back of my mind.

I drink in her face and form.

Kat is wearing the tiny white lace thong I so love, the matching bra, and those spike heels. Right then, I decide I'll make her leave the shoes on as she strips for me.

Why not make it as good as possible since this is the last time, I'll ever see her?

Ready to begin, I shoot her a salute and make my way around the pool to the back door.

It's unlocked, and I slip inside, closing the door quietly behind me.

Thanks to my previous visits with Jason, I am familiar with the layout of the house, so I walk directly to the staircase.

Kat waits at the top of the stairs, one hand resting on the railing at her side.

She is beyond stunning, a fiery angel looking down at me from heaven.

I have the sudden urge to drop to my knees and worship at her feet. I realize I'd never seen her undressed up close. Now I can see all that I'd been missing.

Her skin almost glows. I can see tiny freckles dotting her chest and stomach, and her cheeks blush a beautiful shade of pink. I itch to take photos to relive this moment later, alone, for my pleasure.

But I left my phone in my car, just like she told me to.

Anyway, I don't want to do anything to scare her off. Better to try to secure my own copy of the video later on.

I put up a finger and circle it in the air to let her know I want her to turn for me.

She does, and I am treated to a view of her smooth back, tight ass, and strong thighs and calves.

Those heels are the icing on the cake. They lengthen Kat's legs beautifully, making her calf muscles stand out.

As she turns to face me, I show her that I want her to make another turn for me. She complies. Unable to stand it any longer, I point to her bra and tell her to take it off slowly.

She does, and facing me once more, she raises her hands to the hooks at her back, and a second later, the straps slide from her shoulders, and her bra falls to the floor at her feet.

This. This is what I'd waited for and dreamed about.

No barrier between my eyes and her skin.

She is as perfect as any twenty-something I'd ever watched undress, ripe and lush and blemish-free.

Once again, I have a fleeting wish for my cell phone camera.

I can see Kat trembling, and I know it isn't from the cold. This is difficult for her, but I feel no sympathy. She is the one who led us to this since the first day she took her top off for me.

I breathe heavily, holding the bottom post for support, and I know she can see the effect she has on me.

I wish she would relax and go with it. It would be nice if she isn't so tense.

I have no intention of touching her, as I'd promised.

I don't need to. I'll take what she owes me and split, then meet her husband a few days later and collect my final reward.

I speak. "Now, the rest. But Kat? Leave the shoes on. You know how much I love them."

Kat frowns at this command, and a hint of something new flashes behind her eyes.

Is it anger? Hate? It doesn't matter.

I have her where I want her, and we'll be done here soon.

To my irritation, she breaks the spell. She reminds me of the terms of our deal and asks, again, if I'll be out of her life for good when we are done. I agreed, but now I am annoyed that she'd interrupted my fantasy, the vision I had created for our final moments together.

I need to remind her who is in charge here. "Yes, Kat, I told you this is all I wanted from the beginning. Don't ruin this for me. I want you to take your panties off. You'll do it for me and make it good, or I'll make you touch yourself, too. Now, I'm coming up. I told you I wanted this to end in your bedroom."

I wouldn't follow up on that threat. I just want Kat to get back to the script.

I only want to see her absolutely naked, nothing more, nothing less.

I take it slow, one step at a time, savoring all the details of her body I can see from this close distance.

She backs up a bit as I get closer to allow me room on the landing.

My eyes are locked on her tiny panties at the vee of her legs as I place my foot on the last step.

I am almost there.

The next thing I know, I am tumbling down the stairs, desperately grabbing for something, anything, to break my fall.

My fingers find nothing but air.

The crazy bitch pushed me, I think as I fall.

Then my thoughts are no more.

CHAPTER 69

Grant

I kept quiet while Kat lied to the police.

I understood why she'd told the detective that Tyler had attacked her due to his misplaced and unreciprocated attraction for her.

She obviously couldn't tell them about the game she and Tyler had been playing, so she had to devise a believable reason for him being in the house.

I let her lie to me, too.

I knew why he was really there, but I couldn't let on how I knew, so I let her tell her story the way she wanted.

In the end, I convinced myself it didn't matter. He had gone off course and attacked her and died for it.

That's what is important here, that she isn't blamed.

What I can't understand is how things had gone so horribly wrong. I promised the asshole fifteen thousand goddamn dollars. All he had to do was get Kat to take her clothes off in view of the camera and then disappear. It should have been so simple, but somehow, he'd ended up dead on my hallway floor.

Why had Tyler attacked Kat?

According to her journal entries, he'd never seemed interested in anything but looking at her.

That's why I came up with my plan. I believed she was safe from any harm. He'd also sworn he wouldn't touch her, and I'd thought he was so greedy for the money that he'd have been true to his word.

It is my fault.

He'd have never gone to the house if I hadn't set him up for that goddamn video.

Kat wouldn't be hurt. She wouldn't have had to watch a man die in our house.

I should have given him the money to leave town and left it at that. I was so excited by the prospect of being able to watch what Kat and Tyler had been doing I didn't consider the possibility of it going any way besides the way I'd planned.

That is on me. I am no longer as excited to watch the video. I don't want to watch that madman as he tried to sexually assault my beloved wife. I can't stand the thought of seeing him smash her beautiful face into the wall.

I know the police would have liked to see the video, but Kat had been cleared. I see no reason for anyone to watch my wife be assaulted. No reason for them to watch a man fall to his death. I reason that if the case is ever reopened, I can show them the video as proof of her innocence.

I took two weeks off from work to care for Kat after the incident.

She protested. Kat is usually the one taking care of others, and I think she felt smothered by my attention after the first few days.

I think I ended up staying home to be with her to reassure myself instead of her.

Saturday, two weeks after the assault, I decided to go into the office to catch up on a few things. Angie came over and assures me she'll be with Kat all day.

They are going to make lunch at home and do whatever it is women do when they're alone.

I am nervous about leaving Kat, but she is in good hands. Angie has been a rock since the incident, bringing food and small gifts for Kat almost daily, even taking some time off work to be here.

At the office, I settle into my desk chair. I boot my computer and log into the program for the camera I had hidden in the room.

The camera is gone now. I'd removed it the night of the attack, hiding it deep in my closet until I can get rid of it.

I scroll through the little calendar on the screen and choose the correct date.

The video starts, and I smile. I timed it well.

This first part of the video is fun to watch.

The Window

Kat moves in and out of the frame, from her closet to the bathroom and back, getting ready for Tyler. I watch her apply lotion, rubbing it into her thighs, belly, and breasts. I recognize the bottle. It is one of the scents I love.

She comes out of the bathroom again, this time with her hair curled, and I see her run her hands through it a few times, letting it fall in soft, sexy waves to her shoulders.

I could kick myself for not setting this camera up weeks before. I can watch Kat like this all day.

I start to understand why Tyler is into this voyeur thing. It is mesmerizing to watch. It's like Kat is someone I don't know —just a gorgeous stranger.

On the screen, Kat continues her preparations.

She comes out of the closet, naked, holding a small bundle of something white in her hand.

I use the mouse to zoom in to get a better look at what it is.

The bundle becomes a tiny thong and lacy bra.

She puts the panties on, one leg at a time, and then the bra. I can't tear my eyes away from the screen.

My breath quickens, and I think maybe I'll edit the video for myself, keeping only what happened before Tyler arrived. No one will ever know.

The little clock at the bottom of the video shows eleven o'clock as Kat steps into the window.

I watch, enthralled, as she stands there confidently, the sunlight from the open window kissing her bare skin and turning it golden.

Yes, I definitely understand Tyler better now. I can't see him, but I know he has to be there because she moves to the top of the stairs and waits.

I smile when she stumbles a tiny bit in the tall, tall heels she wore.

From the angle the camera is pointed, I can only see the back of Kat now. I am not let down because she looks as beautiful from the back as she does from the front.

I assume Tyler is downstairs looking up because Kat turns in a slow circle, once and then again.

I imagine him down there giving her instructions, and suddenly I realize I want to do this with her, too.

I decide to let some time pass and let Kat heal physically and mentally before broaching the idea, but I desperately want to play this game with my wife.

A small movement brings me out of my thoughts and back to the screen.

I focus my eyes and see Kat's hands come up behind her back, and she unhooks her bra. I watch as it falls to the floor.

My wife has bared her breasts for Tyler. In our home. In our bedroom.

As far as I know, no one but me has ever seen them. I expect to be angry, but instead, I'm powerfully aroused.

Yes, Kat and I will one day reenact this scene together.

Kat moves, taking two steps back. She must be giving Tyler room to come upstairs as I told him to do.

I want the final scene to be played in full view of the camera, and thus far, it has gone according to plan. Tyler will step into the bedroom next, and she'll take off her panties for him in front of my camera.

Spellbound, I watch. Any minute now, something will change, and Tyler will put his hands on Kat, fight with her, and try to rape her.

I steel myself against how I'll feel when I see that and remind myself that I can't kill Tyler. He is already dead.

The top of Tyler's head appears, then his shoulders come into the camera's view as he climbs the last few steps.

Suddenly, Kat takes two quick steps forward, puts her hands on Tyler's chest, and pushes. In a split second, he disappears from sight.

What the hell?

I reached to press the button to pause the video and then use the mouse to back it up a few seconds.

I watch again as Kat rushes forward and shoves Tyler down the stairs.

I pause the video again.

Rewind. Stop.

Rewind. Stop.

No matter how many times I watch, nothing changes.

My wife killed Tyler. On purpose.

She'd waited until he was off balance at the top of the stairs and then pushed him to his death.

I'm sweating and my hands shake as I sit frozen, not knowing what to do with this information.

Kat is a murderer.

I have to go to the police. They need to know what really happened.

Quickly, I save the video to an empty flash drive and delete it from the camera program, then the trash file, and finally, the server.

I yank the drive from its slot on the computer and shove my chair back, frantically searching for my car keys.

Fumbling with the door key, I finally lock up the office and hurry from the building to the parking lot.

Halfway to my car, I stop short.

Wait a minute. Should I go to the police?

What good would it do me to have Kat in prison?

The answer is none.

Do I want my kids to be labeled as children of a murderess?

Again, no.

Could I somehow use this to my advantage?

Yes, I am beginning to see that I could.

I love my wife despite what I had just watched her do. I want to stay married to her, want to grow old together, and watch our grandchildren grow up with her.

None of that would happen if she spends the rest of her life in jail. And she would.

There is no way to explain the video, no excuse on earth why she was dressed in skimpy lingerie, showing off her body like that before pushing Tyler down the stairs.

She'll go from being perceived as a victim to being branded a cold-blooded killer. Our life as we know it would be over. My children will be shamed. We'll probably have to leave town.

Kat may have had reasons to do what she did, but regardless of what they might be, it's still premeditated murder.

I consider this. If no one other than me sees the video, I hold all the cards. At any time, I can show it to Kat and tell her I know what she's done. She'd basically be bound to do whatever I say for the rest of our lives together.

I won't use it against her unless she gives me cause; unless she gets out of line somehow. Not that I expect her to, but I'll have the video in safekeeping as one more insurance policy.

Just in case.

There is another, greater reason to keep this video to myself.

I am the one who sent Tyler to our house that day. If you think about it, I'm the one who got him killed. Kat had committed the actual murder, but I'd set it up. If I hadn't wanted so badly to watch them play their little game, he'd be alive today.

It's possible I could be charged with negligent homicide or at the very least, an accessory to murder.

If Kat is arrested, my role in the plot would be revealed. What would happen to our kids then?

An hour later, I tuck the flash drive into the pouch with the others in my secret safety deposit box. The cash I had taken out for Tyler also goes back into the box.

Smiling to myself, I pocket the key and leave the bank.

EPILOGUE

Kara

Dear Diary,

They don't know that sometimes when I'm supposed to be at school, I sneak home and hide in the pool house until school lets out.

They don't know that sometimes, when I tell them I'm at soccer practice, I'm hiding, unseen, in the high branches of the neighbor's oak trees.

They don't know that today I spent the day in the tree or that I can see into my mom's bedroom window from up there.

They don't know what I saw my mom do.

Kara.

A Note From The Author

Thanks for reading. I hope you enjoyed my first book!

The sequel to "The Window" is now available for purchase on Kindle Unlimited!

One Last Lie: The Window Duet, Book Two
Eight years ago, Kara witnessed something terrible… and never told anyone.

Now an adult, Kara finds herself without direction, no goals, few friends, and a strained relationship with her parents.

Until a chance meeting changes everything.

Nicole is everything Kara never knew she always wanted. But all is not as it seems. Kara isn't the only one keeping secrets. Torn between family loyalty and a chance at true love, which will Kara choose?

Meanwhile, Kat and Grant each have their own secrets. Years may have passed, but they soon discover that some things never stay buried.